Nora Bonesteel's Christmas Past

Previous Ballad Novels by Sharyn McCrumb

NORA BONESTEEL'S
CHRISTMAS PAST

Sharyn McCrumb

Abingdon fiction™
a novel approach to faith

ISBN-13: 978-1-4267-5421-0
Published by Abingdon Press, P.O. Box 801, Nashville, TN 37202
www.abingdonpress.com

Published in association with the Irene Goodman Literary Agency.

Macro Editor: Teri Wilhelms

Library of Congress Cataloging-in-Publication Data

McCrumb, Sharyn,
  Nora Bonesteel's Christmas past / Sharyn McCrumb.
    pages cm
  ISBN 978-1-4267-5421-0 (binding: jacketed casebound : alk. paper)
1. Christmas stories. I. Title.
  PS3563.C3527N67 2014
  813'.54—dc23

                                                    2014008236

Printed in the United States of America
1 2 3 4 5 6 7 8 9 10 / 19 18 17 16 15 14

With thanks to Officer J. A. Niehaus
and Officer D. J. Runge

1

"Well, it just doesn't seem right, that's all. Arresting somebody on Christmas Eve." Spencer Arrowood shivered as a gust of wind hit him. The fleece-lined glove he had just dug out of the pocket of his nonregulation sheepskin coat spun away from his numb fingers and landed with a little plop in a not-yet-frozen mud puddle beside the curb. With a weary sigh, the sheriff picked it up and flicked at the mud with his hand. "By rights, we ought to be heading home by now."

"Home," Deputy Joe LeDonne shrugged. "Yeah, but it'll be quiet after this, and both the second-shift officers have kids. I figured we might as well let them have the night off.

Martha has gone to visit her sister in Charlotte, so I got no plans. You?"

The sheriff cast a baleful glance to the pewter sky that seemed to stop just above the spire of the courthouse. A few grubby flakes of snow swirled along on the gusts of wind. "Plans? None to speak of. But a few upstanding citizens have invited me to Christmas parties, so I reckoned I'd fetch up somewhere this evening. Maybe make the rounds of three or four of them and make dinner out of the party tray hors d'oeuvres."

"Shall I reserve the drunk tank, Sheriff?"

"Not on my account. I'm sticking to fruit punch."

"Well, good luck with the party circuit. Do any of the invitations sound promising?"

"Well, not for the pleasure of anybody's company, as far as I'm concerned, but there is one from Anna Martha Matuszczyk Kerney." He said the name in one long breath.

"What a mouthful. How did you remember all that?"

Spencer sighed. "It was on the check she wrote for my reelection campaign. I memorized it in case I ever met her. She is the widow of the quarry owner, so I reckon she can afford chocolate-covered quail eggs, or whatever they serve at those fancy parties."

"Champagne and caviar." LeDonne bit back a smile. "Sounds just like your kind of party. You can talk about polo and opera. You gonna change into your tux back at the office?"

Spencer shook his head. "If I had one, they'd probably mistake me for a waiter. And since caviar is just a jumped-up name for fish eggs, maybe I should stick with pigs in a blanket and the vegetable tray and onion dip from Food City."

"You always do," said LeDonne. "Our office Christmas party makes up in consistency what it lacks in creativity. But I do look forward to your mother's chocolate cake every year."

"Clabbered sky," said Spencer, peering up at the clouds. "Looks like it's going to snow here before too long."

The decades-old tinsel and ribbon Christmas decorations, put up by the town of Hamelin on the first Monday in December, swayed in the wind. The narrow main street was empty now; the few little shops closed at noon on Christmas Eve. Anybody with last-minute shopping to do would have headed for Johnson City where the big chain stores never closed at all. Everyone else had gone home to snug brick houses on tree-lined streets or to one of the farmhouses scattered across the valley beneath the dark ridge of mountains, with Christmas trees shining in the living room windows and log fires blazing brightly in the fireplaces.

There was a Christmas tree at the little white house on Elm Avenue, where Spencer's mother still lived; he had bought it and put it up for her two weeks before, but he had not bothered to get one for his own place. He was seldom home, anyhow. LeDonne wouldn't have one, either. He avoided anything with overtones of sentiment, good or bad. The few Christmas cards he received, mostly from local insurance agents and car dealers, went straight in the trash. In any case, he was right: there was no need for either of them to hurry home.

LeDonne slid into the driver's seat of the patrol car. "Well, then, we'd best get it over with before the storm hits. I've already got the warrant. Get in."

The sheriff pulled on the worn leather gloves and wound an old silk aviator scarf around his neck before he took his place in the passenger seat. "It'll be dark in a couple of hours, too. In case this expedition makes me miss the Christmas parties, I hope we can find some place open for supper. I hadn't even finished my sweet potato pie when you hauled me out of Dent's. I suppose this little mission of yours will take us to the back of beyond?"

LeDonne grunted, unmoved by his boss's litany of complaints. "You ought to thank me. I'll bet those party invitations all came from local bureaucrats, and you know you'd hate every minute you had to spend with them. You'd never get enough to eat from the hors d'oeuvre trays, and you might even break your rule and drink too much just to be able to stand the company. So consider this warrant your Christmas gift."

Spencer laughed and caught the folded sheaf of papers the deputy tossed to him. After all the years he and Joe LeDonne had worked together, the deputy knew him well. There was no sense in arguing with the truth. Spencer would have hated those parties. Glad-handing was his least favorite part of the job, and he dreaded every political year as if he were facing a murder trial instead of reelection.

"All right, but this had better not be a wild goose chase on account of some silly misdemeanor. I'm not jailing a litterbug or a jaywalker tonight. Christmas Eve." He unfolded the papers, squinting at the fine print. "Left my reading glasses back on my desk," he muttered. "Does that say Shull?"

"That's right. J. D. Shull. And he's no jaywalker, either."

"Address says Route One. That's out past Dark Hollow." Spencer saw a blank space in the jumble of scrawled writing. "And there's not a phone listing for him, either. No surprise there. I swear that part of the county is only on the map two days a week."

LeDonne did not smile. Because he had not grown up in this place, acquainted with or kin to half the county as Spencer Arrowood was, LeDonne did not share the sheriff's inclination to be friendly to strangers. He gave the benefit of the doubt to no one. The way he saw it, his job was to execute that warrant and to bring in whomever the court had told him to fetch. If there was a misunderstanding to be sorted out or any justice or mercy to be dispensed, that was someone else's responsibility, not part of his duties. He would bring in the prisoner they asked for, and whatever happened after that was not his concern.

"So what did this J. D. Shull do that's so all-fired important that we have to haul him in on Christmas Eve?—And if you tell me he bounced a check, I'm going to be out of this car at the next stop sign."

"Warrant says hit-and-run. He smashed into a car in Knoxville and took off, but somebody got the plate number. Knoxville wants him brought in."

"Anybody killed?"

"Nobody even hurt."

Spencer heaved a weary sigh and shook his head. "Then why in Sam Hill do we have to go out and haul him in on Christmas Eve?"

"That car he hit was a Mercedes belonging to the wife of Senator Robertson."

"And we thought that instead of going back to Florida at Thanksgiving, we would just stay at our place in the mountains and spend Christmas here. Because Christmas has become so commercial in recent years, don't you find?"

Nora Bonesteel smiled politely at her occasional neighbor, Shirley Haverty, who was perched on the chintz sofa in front of Nora's fireplace, attempting to balance a teacup with her silver-lacquered fingernails—they used to be talons, but she'd been forced to trim them when she took up gardening. Shirley had turned up on the doorstep half an hour earlier, resplendent in a turquoise velour tracksuit and rhinestone-studded running shoes. She carried a red-ribboned poinsettia from Food City as a holiday gift for her elderly neighbor in hopes of making her visit seem like a social call.

Nora didn't see Shirley Haverty very often. For more than half of each year, the Havertys lived in Florida, but a few years back, for reasons that were never quite clear to Nora, they had purchased the old farmhouse down the road from her to use as their summer residence. That house, the closest thing Ashe Mountain had to a mansion, was still an imposing structure despite its age and the years it had been neglected.

The Havertys seemed pleasant enough, always waving when they drove past if she was working out in her flower garden, but aside from such casual neighborly gestures, their lives did not touch at any point, and Nora seldom gave them much thought.

Now, though, here was Shirley Haverty, perched on the

old sofa in her parlor like an exotic bird, casting about for topics of conversation. In fact, an exotic bird was exactly what she reminded Nora of. Down past the old barn there was a pond, usually occupied by a few white farm ducks and an occasional itinerant mallard, but during the spring and autumn bird migrations, more exotic creatures, heading to or from their winter nesting grounds, would make rest stops in the ponds and streams all along the path of the mountains, which they used as a celestial Warriors' Path to guide them on their seasonal north/south journeys. At such times, a regal blue heron—Nora thought it might always be the same one— stopped in the duck pond in the same week of every April and October. It was a magical-looking creature with legs like corn stalks and smoky blue-gray feathers, just the color of the distant mountains at twilight. The heron would stay around the pond for a few days, resting from its long flight and scarfing down whatever fish it could find, and then it would take wing again, heading for the southern tropics in autumn or the austere woodlands of Canada in spring. It never stayed long, and it never took any notice of the local waterfowl, dwarfed by its size and eclipsed by its magnificence. The shabby, earthbound farm ducks would huddle together at the edge of the pond, gaping at the lordly newcomer as if he were a visiting prince. They never challenged the heron or confronted it at all, and it ignored them as if they were no more than rocks at the water's edge. The pond ducks simply waited in strained silence until the heron decided to leave again, and then things settled back to normal as if he had never been there at all.

The summer people were like that. They showed up for a little while each year, aloof and exotic, mostly taking no notice of the local community, and then one day they'd be gone again. Their presence didn't trouble Nora. Their paths rarely crossed, because the summer people didn't show up in church, and Nora did not frequent the outlet mall or the wine and cheese parties favored by her erstwhile neighbors. The locals who became acquainted with them were mostly those who had to: the plumbers, the carpenters, the cabinetmakers.

Nora might have gone on peacefully coexisting and serenely unaware of the Havertys' existence, except that early in the summer, Shirley Haverty had decided to take up gardening.

Inspired by a lecture on local plant lore she had attended down at the college, a course open to the general community,

Shirley had come away enchanted with the idea of creating art with landscaping. She had hopes of making the dull and ordinary front yard of their summer place into a haven for native plants and wildflowers. The accompanying slide show depicting such a garden had been inspiring in a general way, but time and a barrage of questions had prevented the lecturer from going into detail about just how to accomplish this feat. But Shirley was inspired; shortly after that lecture she had started asking around for local guidance in native gardening, and somewhere between the Hamelin nursery and the farmers' market, one of the local residents had told her about Nora Bonesteel.

A few days later Shirley had showed up on the doorstep of Nora's white-frame house one morning in a scarf-tied straw hat, yellow polo shirt and khaki shorts, and espadrilles. She had handed Nora a personal check and a gift basket of soaps and lotions from the mall's bath and body store, and announced, "I have come so that you can teach me how to garden."

Still bemused at this unsubtle encounter, Nora told this story a few days later to her old friend Jane Arrowood, who stopped in for tea.

Jane's eyes widened. "And you let her in? Did you really? I think I would have torn up the check in her face, thrown the gift basket back at her, and pushed her off the porch."

Nora smiled. "Well, I never did cash the check. It's in the drawer of the lamp table. But I might use the soaps she brought; I'm partial to the smell of lavender. I am also partial to gardening, and I decided it wouldn't do any harm to listen to what the woman wanted. Perhaps we owe it to the world to teach others some of what we know. Anyhow, it is kind of a tradition around here, if you think about it. Remember Lydia Bean?"

Jane nodded. "Tennessee history. If my memory of eighth grade doesn't fail me, Lydia Bean was a young settler's wife, kidnapped from around here by a Cherokee war party in the late 1700s, and they were getting ready to burn her at the stake when the tribe's wise woman intervened."

"Yes. Her rescuer was the famous *Ghighau*, Nancy Ward. They say she stamped out the fire herself and saved Mrs. Bean's life by making her promise to teach the Cherokee women how to make butter and cheese. The captive agreed, of course, and after a few weeks' instruction, they let her go home."

NORA BONESTEEL'S CHRISTMAS PAST

"Well, I wouldn't put it past the summer people to start burning us at the stake," sighed Jane, "but I think they see it the other way around. They seem to think *we're* the savages. They're intent on taking our land, which makes me feel like a Cherokee anyhow. But it's one thing to teach folks a skill in order to escape a bonfire and quite another to do it for a basket of perfumed soap and hand lotion."

Nora smiled. "Oh, it wasn't that, Jane. I chalked my teaching her up to Christian charity. It turns out Shirley Haverty is not a bad sort once you get to know her, and besides, I'd like to see an old-fashioned garden at the Honeycutt place again. It used to be so pretty there when I was a girl."

The Honeycutts had been gone for decades, the older generation dead and the younger ones married, moved away, and now elderly themselves, but local people still called the sprawling two-story place in a meadow on Ashe Mountain "the Honeycutt place" even though almost no one now remembered the original owners. Nora did, though. She remembered summer ice cream parties on the lawn—made with cream from the neighbors' cows and fresh berries picked from the bushes down by the creek, all packed together with salt and ice in a hand-cranked contraption that seemed to take forever, but it made the best ice cream she'd ever tasted.

The Honeycutts. How long ago that was.

In other seasons, there had been neighborhood dances sometimes in the big parlor. A few of the young people danced, while Judge Honeycutt and a couple of other neighbors played fiddle and mandolin—old tunes, like "Shady Grove" and "Down by the Willow Garden"—none of that new jitterbug or jazz music you could hear on the radio back then. The judge did not approve of the newfangled dance crazes. He was a kind man, though, and now and then when times were hard and crops had suffered from the weather, many a family up on the mountain had found a bag of store-bought necessities on their doorstep or a box of homemade jams and canned beans from Miss Ida's pantry. He never offered those gifts in person, though, for it would have embarrassed both the giver and the receiver to be caught in the act of charity.

Judge Honeycutt had died after a long, full life, just on the eve of the election of President Kennedy. Nora had mourned his passing, along with the rest of the community, but years later looking back on it, she thought it might have been fitting

NORA BONESTEEL'S CHRISTMAS PAST

that his end had come in conjunction with the era he had belonged to. His gentle old-fashioned ways were not suited to the brash modern world, and the judge would have been saddened to live on as a stranger in a harsher time. Miss Ida had followed her husband to the grave a couple of winters later, and the house went to their last surviving son. Two sons had died in infancy, and the older boy was killed in the Battle of the Bulge. Seven years later, the last surviving son, Rob, had left home to serve in the Korean War. While he was in the army, he had met and married a girl "from away" and attended a Pennsylvania college on the GI bill. By the time Rob Honeycutt inherited the house, his life was firmly rooted elsewhere, and so the place stayed vacant year after year with just a local handyman around to see to its upkeep. After perhaps a decade of this, the younger Honeycutts—strangers to the mountains—felt no attachment to the old home place, and the house was sold. Since then it had passed through a number of tenants and owners until finally the Havertys bought it, hoping to restore the property to its former glory.

The Honeycutt place was a white farmhouse, three stories high—not small or inexpensive, but spare and of simple design. Set between the blacktopped country road and the forest behind it, it nestled in a meadow below the sharp ridge of the mountain. A dry stone wall lined the gravel driveway, and the covered porch was sheltered by old lilac bushes growing untrimmed and untended on either side of the front steps.

"I was glad for the chance to speak to her about gardens," Nora told Jane Arrowood. "They have been making changes to the house, painting it and putting in picture windows, and so on, and before they got around to rearranging the yard, I wanted to tell her how many years it takes for lilacs to reach that size."

Jane nodded. "Longer than any of us would live to see them get that big. Cutting them down would be a sin. Did she listen?"

"Oh, yes. She seemed pleased to be told."

"Well, then," said Jane, "you'll probably save some lives."

"How do you mean?"

"Well, those new people haven't any notion at all of what plants will grow up here, and the ones I know are always sending away for camellias and trying to plant ficus hedges, which work very well five hundred miles southeast of here, but three thousand feet up in east Tennessee, they just fall over dead." She smiled. "I suppose it would be a kindness for you to spare the lives of a few helpless camellias, though no doubt these summer people can afford any amount of replacements."

"I expect they could. When she gave me that check, she didn't have any notion at all that she might be giving offense, and I didn't want to hurt her feelings by correcting her. She's right about the garden, though. Now that they are restoring the house, the grounds do need to be tended as well, and the garden should be in keeping with the house."

"As opposed to, say, a cactus garden?" Jane smiled and shook her head. *Summer people.*

Nora nodded. "Yes, I'd like to see the old plants restored to the Honeycutts' garden, and that wouldn't happen unless somebody gave the present owner some advice. I suppose I'm doing it in memory of the Honeycutts as much as anything. The judge and Miss Ida were fine people, and they loved that house.

"Anyhow, I don't mind telling her what plants she'll need and how to take care of them. I even gave her some cuttings and extra bedding plants from here to get her started, and she's good about doing the digging and planting herself. I might have been less accommodating if she had intended to hire a gardener and sit back while somebody else did all the work. But she wants to landscape the place herself—said the exercise was good for her heart—and I'd like to see her get it right."

Jane Arrowood shook her head. "No good deed goes unpunished, Nora. I hope you don't end up with a yard full of summer people in golf shorts and running shoes, all wanting you to supervise their lawn projects. Even Lydia Bean only spent a few weeks instructing the Cherokee women. I doubt you'd get off that lightly."

Nora twisted her hands in her lap. "Well, you're right about that, Jane. Things have already taken a turn I hadn't quite bargained for."

"What do you mean?"

"Shirley Haverty stopped by again this morning. She was so agitated I could barely make out what the matter was, and it wasn't gardening that had set her off."

"Why, what happened?"

"She claims the house is haunted."

2

Spencer Arrowood tapped his fingers on the steering wheel. His frown deepened. "So we have to go to the back of beyond on Christmas Eve just because some old boy put a dent in the senator's wife's Mercedes?"

LeDonne grunted. "Which would you rather do: serve this warrant or go to a champagne-and-fish-eggs party with the senator? Tell the truth."

"Well, that's not much of a choice. Why didn't you include hitting my thumb with a hammer? That might beat out both of them."

"The drive will be the longest part of the deal, Spencer. Once we get out there, we'll arrest the guy, put him in the

25

back of the squad car—five minutes, tops—and drive back to town. Then you can get on with the glad-handing and the hors d'oeuvre eating, and I'll get a cheeseburger on the way home."

Nothing in the way LeDonne said it indicated self-pity, but the sheriff felt a pang of guilt anyhow. "Look, Joe, you shouldn't be alone for the holidays. My mother always does the whole turkey dinner extravaganza, even though there's just the two of us. Why don't you come by her house tomorrow afternoon and join us?"

LeDonne nodded. "Maybe I will." But they both knew that he wouldn't.

Spencer looked up at the gray clouds that seemed to drift lower by the minute. "You know, your timetable might be a tad optimistic, Joe. From the look of that sky, we could end up spending the holiday with—what's his name?"

"Shull. There's a slew of them out in the Ashe Mountain district."

"Well, there would be, Joe. There was a Shull among the settlers at Robertson's fort in 1776—before Tennessee *was* Tennessee."

"Well, let's see which one this is." LeDonne squinted at the printing on the warrant. "Shull, J. D."

"Never heard of him."

"Well, Sheriff, coming from you, that's a good sign, isn't it?"

"I expect it is. I just hope we don't get stranded out there. Steep, one-lane mountain road. Houses with central heating are few and far between out that way. *The Little Match Girl* is not my favorite Christmas story."

LeDonne pondered the connection between central heating and a Christmas story. "Is that the one about the kid who froze to death in the alley? I don't know who wrote it, but it didn't happen anywhere around here, I guarantee you."

"No. It's Hans Christian Andersen, so I reckon it's Denmark. I hope you're right about it never happening around here. That would suit me just fine as a Christmas present: a day in which nobody gets arrested and nobody dies."

Nora Bonesteel set the refilled teapot on the cherrywood table beside the sofa. In the grate, oak logs blazed and crackled merrily, making fire music to accompany the conversation. "I'm surprised to see you here this late in the year," she told her visitor. "Don't you usually go back to Florida when the last leaf falls."

Shirley Haverty shook her head. "I wanted it to feel like Christmas. The way it is in the movies, I mean. *White Christmas, Christmas in Connecticut . . .*" she sighed, perhaps captivated by visions of snowflakes and sleigh bells dancing in her head. "You know, there aren't really any seasons in Florida, and when one of our neighbors told us that the really harsh winter weather doesn't start here in Tennessee until late January, I started to think about staying on. She must have been right. The temperatures now are still above freezing and there hasn't been a snowfall."

Nora glanced out the big window that overlooked the back-yard of the farmhouse, where a hundred yards from the back porch the ground fell away to the patchwork of fields and woods in the valley below and beyond that a wall of mountains stretching away to the horizon. Today, though, skeins of gray clouds hovered low, obscuring the view.

"The winter does tend to settle in after the new year," said

Nora. "But it's not an ironclad rule. I can remember when we had snows in late October. Not lately, though."

Shirley Haverty nodded. "Bill says it's global warming. Anyhow, I thought we'd chance it. We've owned our mountain house for three years now, but we always left after Thanksgiving and didn't come back until Easter. Last winter, though, I asked Bill if we could stay on for Christmas this year. He sold the company and retired a few years ago, so there's no reason we have to go back at a specific time. I thought it would be nice to see the house in the winter for a change. He said we could." She blushed. "I knew he would agree, so when we came up last spring, I brought along all our Christmas decorations from Florida."

Nora smiled as she handed her guest a plate of iced sugar cookies shaped as snowmen, candy canes, and bells. "I expect you'll be all right this year. I've seen the Honeycutt house— that is, your place now—decorated for the holidays. It looks like a scene from a Christmas card."

"Well, that's what I thought," said Shirley, nodding happily. "I was even hoping for a dusting of snow to complete the picture. Bill and I put up some of the decorations two days ago.

That's what started it, really. The trouble I came to tell you about."

"Started the trouble?"

"Yes. In all the time we've owned that house—three years; well, I told you that—it has always seemed peaceful. A happy house, you know . . . that is, if houses can have feelings."

"Oh, I think they can," Nora murmured.

"That's why I was more surprised than frightened when things began to happen."

Nora Bonesteel sat very still. After a moment's pause, she said, "What things?"

Shirley gulped a deep breath and went on. "I hope you won't think I'm going crazy, Miz Bonesteel."

Shirley had called her mountain neighbor "Nora" just once, and she in turn was always addressed as "Mrs. Haverty." It took some getting used to, because the urban world these days seems to think that using first names, even among strangers, is "friendly." When she noticed that the mountain community did not embrace this new practice, she thought their absence of familiarity might indicate a rejection, but the people didn't seem unkind or unhelpful; just . . . formal.

Finally, she asked one of the locals about it at the Saturday farmers' market. "We tend not to be pushy up here, ma'am," the elderly farmer told her. "A lot of us, especially the older folks, feel like calling scant acquaintances by their first names is a little bit like trespassing. We don't go where we're not invited. Speaking for myself, ma'am, when people start first-naming me the minute I meet them, I feel like I'm being pushed into a closeness I didn't agree to."

Shirley gave a lot of thought to the farmer's explanation, and finally she decided that the mountain people needed more space than city dwellers: a few acres between houses and perhaps a neutral zone around themselves, too. They might let you in and be the most loyal friend in creation, but until they did *invite you in, you had to respect the boundaries.*

When Shirley worked all this out, she said to her husband, "You know, I finally understand that Robert Frost poem: 'Good fences make good neighbors.' People must be the same way up in rural New England, where he was from." Bill smiled at her and nodded. "Different accents, same folks," he told her. "I'll bet the Japanese would think they were the only people over here with any manners."

31

Now Shirley Haverty was running her finger around the rim of her teacup and looking big with news, but not one bit happy about it.

In the reassuring tone she adopted when speaking to nervous animals and little children, Nora said, "Oh, I don't believe I'll think you're crazy, Mrs. Haverty. A lot of strange things seem to happen in these mountains that wouldn't happen anywhere else. Just tell me what has upset you."

Shirley nodded and plunged into her story, but frightened or not, she never could get to the point for a good five minutes. Nora sat back with her hands folded in her lap, patiently listening.

"Well, first we put up the Christmas tree in the living room. That was on Sunday. And while we were trimming the tree, Bill put on some Christmas music."

Nora nodded, and remembering her guest's recent raptures about an old-fashioned Christmas, she ventured a guess. "Mr. Bing Crosby, would that be?"

"'White Christmas', you mean? Well, no. We don't really have any traditional holiday music; none that we brought up here, anyway, but Bill saw a seasonal CD on sale in the drugstore last week, so he bought it and put it on to set the mood. It's an old collection of funny Christmas songs. 'Jingle Bell Rock,' 'Santa Baby,' 'Grandma Got Run Over by a Reindeer,' the Chipmunks' Christmas song . . ." Seeing her neighbor's bewildered expression, she explained, "Light, cheery tunes. Comical songs. Well, anyhow, we put on that CD, and I got out our collection of ornaments, and we spent most of the afternoon trimming the tree."

Nora smiled. "I remember Judge Honeycutt always used to have a big old Scotch pine set up in the front hall. That tree was about as big around as it was tall, so the top of it went way up into the stairwell. You'd have to go upstairs to see the angel on the top of it. To decorate the tree, the Honeycutts would invite all the young people in the community and a few of the Honeycutt boys' friends from school to a big Christmas party. We'd sit in the parlor talking to one another while the local fiddlers played the old songs from the mountains, and as we talked, we made the decorations for the tree: paper chains, strings of popcorn, and little dolls out of cloth and clothespins. We used yarn for the hair." Nora smiled at the memory. "They also had a set of beautiful ornaments, hand-carved out

of cherrywood. A rocking horse, a star, a horn, an angel . . .
One of the Jessups was a woodworker, and he made them.
One every year for a dozen years or so, until he died, which
was right around the time of the War." Nora sighed. "I wonder
what became of those ornaments."

"I wish I could tell you," said Shirley. "I'd love to see them.
They weren't in the attic or the outbuilding, though. We
looked through all the old boxes up there just after we bought
the house. Maybe someone in the present generation of the
family has them."

"Pardon me, I was woolgathering," said Nora, wresting her
attention back to the present. "Talking about the Honeycutt
house took me back to the Christmas parties they used to
hold there before the War." Shirley knew that by *the War*, Miz
Bonesteel meant World War II. Everybody her age did. "They
stopped giving the parties after Tom. . . . Well, never mind. It
was all a long time ago."

But again, the past occupied her thoughts. "Yes, it was never
quite the same once the War started. Those parties they had
when the boys were still with us, those were special times. After
the musicians had played enough old tunes to tire themselves

out, they would quit and head for the buffet table. That's when the judge would put down his fiddle and lead the carol singing around the piano. They served hot cider made from the apples in their orchard, and one of Miss Ida's fruitcakes. And there was a big silver platter heaped with gingerbread men and store-bought chocolate candy. After the refreshments, we young folks played parlor games with little trinkets for prizes."

Shirley nodded and smiled, but she had a hard time picturing Nora Bonesteel as a young woman.

"I still have a blue glass-bead necklace I won one year. They blindfolded us one at a time, and we had to throw a dart at a paper donkey. I came closest to the target, and I remember my cousin Sarah said it wasn't fair for me to win, because even blindfolded, she reckoned that I . . . Well, never you mind. Those were fine times." Nora took a deep breath, banishing the old memories, and turned back to her guest. "Now you were telling me that something strange happened while you were trimming your Christmas tree."

"Something really strange, Miz Bonesteel, but it wasn't while we were decorating the tree. It was after that. The tree trimming went along just fine. Bill managed to untangle the lights and string them on the tree, and we finished about seven, had our dinner, and watched a little television before we went to bed. Everything was fine then. I am certain about that, because before we went upstairs, I went back into the living room to turn off the lights, but before I did, I took another peek at the finished tree. It was just like we left it."

"Did something happen in the night?"

"Well, I suppose it must have, but we slept right through it. Didn't hear a thing. But when we got up the next morning, I went straight to the kitchen to start breakfast, and Bill wandered into the living room, thinking he'd play the Christmas CD again. Next thing I knew, I heard him yelling for me, and I took the skillet off the burner and rushed in there, thinking he had taken ill. But that wasn't it. When I got to the doorway, I saw Bill standing there, just staring at the demolished Christmas tree. It had been knocked over, so there it lay right in the middle of the rug, like a dead body. Just laid out. And we also had to stick some of the branches back on." Seeing Nora's bewildered expression, Shirley said, "Didn't I mention that? We have an aluminum tree, shrimp pink, about six feet tall, and you can take it apart, so it made it easy to get it up here from our house in Florida."

As she talked, Nora's gaze went past her to the picture window. Beyond the lawn of sere brown grass and the checkered fields in the valley, she could see row after row of hazy blue mountains. The hardwoods on the slopes had shed their leaves for the winter, but interspersed among the bare branches of the oaks and maples were patches of dark green. The pines and the fir trees stayed green all year long. She supposed that was why people had chosen them as symbols for a celebration that takes place in the dead of winter. They were a reminder and a promise that spring would come again.

"Our ornaments weren't on the branches anymore, either," Shirley Haverty was saying. "Most of them were scattered all over the room as if somebody had just flung them every which way at random. And one of the blown-glass ones—the pink flamingo—had been smashed into a dozen pieces. It was my favorite one, and we had to throw it away."

"The pink flamingo," Nora murmured. "*White Christmas*, I believe you said you wanted?"

Shirley blushed. "I know: it's a contradiction. That's what

Bill says—he's always telling me that I say one thing, and then go and do something entirely different. But it makes sense to me, anyhow. I mean, it was the spirit of the holiday I was trying to capture, and honestly, after we settled in here for the winter, I began to think I couldn't manage a traditional Christmas the way they show it in TV movies. For one thing, I wouldn't have the first idea how to make a fruitcake."

"Well, it's too late for you to start one this year, anyway." Nora thought of the long-ago holidays, when the fruitcake sat on a shelf in Grandma Flossie's pantry from the week after Thanksgiving until a few days before Christmas: a confection full of pecans, dates, candied fruit bits, and raisins, wrapped in cheesecloth and soaked in wine. Not many people went to that much trouble anymore. She sighed and returned to the present. "What did you have instead, Mrs. Haverty? For your Christmas decorations, I mean."

"You mean, besides the pink flamingo?" Shirley was smiling. "Yes, I'm sure it sounds peculiar to you, but remember what I told you—we don't really have seasons in south Florida—so instead of getting ornaments of snowmen and reindeer and icicles—you know, things we couldn't really relate to—we decided to collect ornaments more in keeping with our tropical locale. We had the pink flamingo and a Santa Claus in shorts and a Hawaiian shirt. Big ornaments made to look like ripe oranges. And, let's see . . . a manatee, some palm trees, angelfish, and half a dozen green glass alligators. It was just the most festive-looking tree you can imagine, and now it's ruined. Beyond repair. And we'll never find ornaments like those around here."

"I don't imagine you will," Nora said solemnly.

"No, I didn't think so. And it's too late to get them by mail order." She shook her head sadly. "Well, anyhow, Miz Bonesteel, the tree was a shambles. The first thing we did was to check all the doors and windows, because we were sure that somebody had broken in during the night. But all the doors were locked, and not a single window had been broken or tampered with, so we couldn't figure out how anybody could have got inside. We haven't given a spare house key to anybody."

"Did you call the sheriff and report it?"

Shirley shook her head. "We thought about it, but nothing was taken. Bill's wallet was right on the dresser where he'd put it the night before, and there was a pocketful of loose change in the silver bowl on the hall table. We spent an hour going over every room in the house, and we didn't find a single thing missing. Bill said he'd feel foolish calling the police to report a fallen Christmas tree."

Nora smiled. "I've known Sheriff Arrowood since he was knee-high to a grasshopper, and he's as good a man as you'll find, but you may be right. He might not put much store in a complaint about a Christmas tree being knocked over and nothing stolen. As likely as not, he'd tell you that the tree was felled by a gust of wind from an open door or some such explanation."

"Yes, that's exactly what Bill said. He came up with the gust-of-wind theory, too, and I think he had himself three-quarters of the way convinced that it really did happen that way. But I didn't believe it for a second. I thought it might be local teenagers up to mischief. But, as I said, there were no signs of a break-in, and I didn't think kids could get in without leaving any trace that they'd been there."

Nora nodded. "It doesn't seem likely. There are boys in these parts with meanness in them, but they don't live anywhere near you, and I don't think they'd leave without taking something."

"I know. We never did make sense of it, but finally we just accepted it as a freak accident. Bill said that sometimes around here there are little earthquakes so slight that people don't even feel them. He thought that might be it."

"Yes, people like to know the reasons for things. It makes them feel better somehow."

"I suppose it does. Bill cheered up a lot after he fixed on the earthquake theory. Anyhow, he and I spent the morning putting the tree to rights and hanging the ornaments back on the branches. But there was something peculiar about that, too."

Nora sat very still for a moment, keeping her expression carefully neutral. "Something else happened?"

"Well, it may just be a coincidence, of course. That's what Bill says. But you remember the holiday CD I told you we bought? The one with the comic songs. Well, Bill put it on the CD player, so that we'd have music to listen to while we worked. But the CD player wouldn't work. He'd take the CD out and fiddle with all the controls, thinking he'd had the volume set too low or something. But everything seemed fine. It just wouldn't make a sound. We ended up turning on the radio, but all we found on the dial was a lecture on farming and a country music station." She sighed. "It just wasn't the same."

"No, I suppose not, but aside from the broken ornaments, there was no real harm done, was there?"

"I'm just coming to that. After we finished putting the tree back the way it was before, Bill and I went to town for groceries. It was broad daylight, mind you; maybe two o'clock, but nowhere near dusk, even for an overcast winter afternoon. We must have been gone a couple of hours, because we also went to the post office; then we had coffee and pie at Dent's Café, and before we went home we stopped for gas. It was still light when we got back to the house—that sort of dim late-afternoon light you get near the end of December, but still bright enough to see clearly. From outside, everything looked fine. The house was all shut and locked, just the way we left it, with the pine wreath on the door and the hall light on."

Shirley paused for breath and looked at Nora with a worried frown. "You won't believe it, Miz Bonesteel."

Nora smiled. "I expect I will, Mrs. Haverty. You don't strike me as a fanciful person. Go on and tell me what happened."

"We went inside, and while Bill was hanging up our coats I went into the living room to turn the lights on. When Bill heard me scream, he came running. The Christmas tree had fallen again. Ornaments scattered around, but mostly they ended up beside that built-in bookcase beside the fireplace. They just seemed to roll there—an uneven floor, perhaps."

Nora remembered the bookcase, a walnut cabinet stretching from floor to ceiling, but she said nothing.

"And before Bill could put the blame on his earthquake or gust-of-wind theory, I pointed to the mantelpiece. We had received about a dozen Christmas cards, and that morning I set them standing upright all the way across the mantelpiece. *And they were still there!* Not a one of them had fallen over, but the tree was down. We left it lying there on the floor, because I just couldn't bear it if that Christmas tree got knocked over again, and Bill didn't even try to come up with an explanation this time. I was so afraid I hardly slept a wink last night for worrying about it, so this morning I came to see you, and I want you to tell me the truth, Miz Bonesteel. Is our house haunted?"

Nora sat still for a moment before she spoke, "Well, Mrs. Haverty, it didn't used to be."

As the patrol car began its climb up the mountain to Dark Hollow, the two-lane blacktop road narrowed and lost its painted center line. Thick pine trees formed a curtain on both sides of the road, blocking any view there might have been from the steep mountainside. When they reached the highest point of the road, the car entered a thick white mist, making it difficult to see anything except a few yards of the road ahead. Tourists often mistook that dense haze for fog, but it wasn't. Near the top of the mountain, low-hanging rain clouds, level with the land at this altitude, drifted across the road, making an impenetrable curtain of mist. When the car had crested the ridge and started back down the other side, the road would be clear again.

"Take it easy here, Joe." The sheriff, who had seen this phenomenon all his life, knew to slow down to a crawl when the clouds covered the road, because the car could crash into a deer or a stalled vehicle ahead before the driver even saw it. LeDonne had turned on the headlights, putting them on the low setting; high beams would simply bounce off the mist, making it even more opaque and harder to see through.

"Here's our white Christmas, Deputy," said the sheriff.

LeDonne grunted, keeping his eyes on the road. "I hope we don't have much farther to go. I don't want to be fogbound on this road after dark, if we can help it."

"The Shull place is supposed to be somewhere a mile or so from here. I'll read the mailboxes."

"If you can see them."

"Well, at least they're not fine print. I'm all right with distance. Anyhow, there haven't been any mailboxes yet."

"Well, as slow as we're going, you'll have time to read the mailboxes *and* the mail."

"I'll tell you one thing, Joe. That senator who insisted we come out here for a fender-bender—he's lost my vote."

They crept along the cloud-laden road, with only an occasional tree trunk or roadside boulder standing out from the shroud of haze. Minutes later the road curved downward, descending the mountain in a series of corkscrew bends. By the time they had dropped a hundred feet lower than the crest of the mountain, the mist was gone and the clouds were once more in the sky above their heads. They were still in the wilderness, though, bounded on both sides by thick groves of trees, and bordered by steep barren cliffs that had been cut in the 1930s when the road builders blasted their way across the mountain to blaze a trail wide enough for automobiles.

Another hundred feet took them out of the woods and past empty fields of dry grass. At quarter-mile intervals, they began to pass the graveled driveways leading to the small farms set well back across the road opposite the steep sloping side of the mountain. At the entrance to each farm road, they saw battered metal mailboxes, mounted on wooden posts, standing at car-window height along the grass verge. They were positioned so that the mailman could fill the boxes without getting out of his car. Each mailbox was marked with a name or a house number, but over the years the lettering had been worn away by the elements. The owners did not bother to refurbish them, though; the mailman and anybody likely to come calling knew who lived where.

Spencer began by reading off the names or numbers as they went past each mailbox, "Johnson . . . Box 109 . . . Fletch—I guess that's supposed to be Fletcher . . ." His voice trailed off with a weary sigh. "It would take a mind-reader to decipher some of these . . ."

"I'll slow down some more," said LeDonne, suiting the action to the words. "It'll be quicker than having to drive up and down this road a few more times until you spot the right one."

"Shull!" The sheriff announced triumphantly. "Got it. No box number, but the last name is clear enough. Turn here at the driveway—or whatever you call a mile-long stretch of gravel that leads to a farmhouse."

LeDonne eased the car off the asphalt road and onto the narrow lane that led to the Shull farm. A few yards in, the car began to lurch and dip in and out of red clay ruts, where a year of rain had washed away the gravel.

"Feels like you're driving over a washboard, doesn't it, Joe? I suppose they don't see any point in fixing it until spring. The winter rains would just wash it out again."

"I reckon these folks don't get out much."

"Well, they must leave every now and then," said Spencer, "because the complaint puts Mr. Shull in Knoxville last week."

"I wonder what he was doing way down there. I doubt they'd need anything out of the expensive mall stores. These are the folks who'd buy their Sunday clothes at Walmart."

Spencer smiled. "And before Walmart they would have ordered what they needed out of the Wish Book." He didn't need to explain to LeDonne that *the wish book* was the old rural name for the Sears Roebuck catalogue. Back in the days when a trip to town was an all-day excursion, most people who lived out in the country ordered everything from overalls to Christmas toys from that catalogue, six inches thick and filled with pictures of the merchandise they carried. Up until the 1940s you could even buy a house from Sears, and they'd ship it to you in crates, ready to assemble.

"He could have been Christmas shopping," said LeDonne. "But my guess would be that he had some sort of medical appointment with a specialist." He left the word *cancer* unspoken, as if the very mention of it could bring it down on them.

"I'm just glad the county will be paying for the shock absorbers and the wheel alignment, because this car is going to need it after this."

Behind them, the mist was still lingering on the peak above, but despite the clear visibility here, the gray clouds hovered thick and low, putting a lid on the barren landscape. The rutted road twisted and turned, perhaps following the course of the rock-studded creek that ran through the property. They couldn't see the farmhouse yet, only brown fields of high grass stretching away to woods on either side. One lone deer was browsing in the far field. It looked up to watch them as they drove past, and then lowered its head again and returned its attention to the grass.

In another quarter mile, past a stand of pines and a few more bends in the road, they saw the farmhouse, a two-story, white-frame dwelling with a sagging porch and a tin roof of rusty patchwork. The house had seen better days. The gabled box probably dated from the early twentieth century when it might have cost a thousand dollars to build. Nowadays, you couldn't even paint it for that sum, though, and the house certainly needed it. The two spreading oak trees in the front yard looked older than the house. Set between them, a truck tire, painted white, enclosed a now-barren flower bed.

LeDonne stopped the patrol car fifty yards from the house and sat for a moment sizing up the property.

Spencer hit the dashboard with the flat of his hand. "I hate politics!"

LeDonne shrugged. "Who doesn't?"

3

"You didn't have to pick me up," said Nora. "I could have walked. It's only a mile or so." She paused uncertainly beside the passenger door of Shirley Haverty's white Cadillac.

"Walk? Why, it's freezing out here, Miz Bonesteel." Although Shirley wore a parka, an East Tennessee State toboggan hat, and leather gloves, she was shivering, and her nose and cheeks were red from the cold. "I guess you must be used to the cold, but I doubt if I ever will be. Honestly, sometimes in these mountains I even get chilled in mid-July. But on the way here my dashboard thermometer said 38 degrees, and there's no arguing with that. And the wind feels like a chainsaw."

Nora Bonesteel smiled. "You should have seen the winters we had when I was a girl."

"I'll take your word for it." She settled herself behind the wheel and waited for her passenger to fasten her seat belt. "Well, never mind. We'll be warm in a couple of minutes. The first thing we did when we bought the house was to install central heating, and I keep the thermostat turned up to eighty degrees. Bill fusses, but I tell him that we're of an age when you feel the cold more than young people do." She glanced at Nora, who was years older than they were. Instead of a coat, she wore a red woolen shawl over a long-sleeved gray dress, and she had no hat or gloves.

Nora smiled and answered her unspoken thought. "I would have wrapped up more if I were going to walk to your house, but it's a short walk from a warm house to a warm car. I don't mind the little bit of cold in between."

"I'm so grateful to you for coming over, Miz Bonesteel. It will be a treat to have some company." Shirley wasn't sure what the etiquette was for consulting a psychic, if that's what the old lady was, and in her invitation to visit their house she was careful to make no mention of it. Nora Bonesteel certainly wasn't one of those professional fortune-tellers with a neon sign in the window and a made-up name like "Madame Lorayne." They had a fair few of those types in the shabbier neighborhoods back in Florida, frauds preying upon the credulous and the desperate, but Nora Bonesteel was nothing like them.

Shirley would never have known that her neighbor had "the Sight," as they called it up here in the mountains, except for the fact that one of the other summer people had mentioned it one day at a get-together. The woman had heard it from her cleaning lady. *"She knows things," the woman had told her employer. "Sometimes she can tell what's going to happen. They say that when she was a little girl, she saw wreaths and a coffin at the church altar—but everybody told her there was nothing there. Three days later, though, the wreaths and the coffin were right where she said they'd be. But Nora Bonesteel knew about it before the woman even died. After she grew up she would turn up with a stew or a homemade cake just a day before there's a death in the family, while the rest of the community had to wait to show sympathy until after it happens. As far as anybody can tell, she doesn't mean to show off by bringing the food a day too early; it's like she has trouble with the present and the future—she has a*

hard time keeping them straight. But she never foretells anything
for anybody; never tells who is marked for death.

"Now, Miss Nora, she don't like to talk about her gift at all,
and, Lord-a-mercy, don't you never ask her to show it off, and
never, never try to offer her money for anything she does for you.
She'd be civil to you, I reckon, but she would be mortally offended
all the same. Miss Nora don't do foolishness like messing with
fortune-telling cards or crystal balls, and you won't catch her giv-
ing advice to the lovelorn. But all the same she knows things, and
sometimes she'll have a quiet word with somebody, even if they
don't know that they need help. But you can't hire her or nothin'.
She's as independent as a hog on ice. I reckon she has her own
rules about what she'll do and what she won't, and you'll not
budge her from those rules for love nor money."

Shirley Haverty had found this local lore quite intriguing.
Listening to the tale of her neighbor's mysterious talents gave
her the same shivery feeling she'd had once on a ghost walk
in Edinburgh. At the time, though, the information about
her mysterious neighbor did not concern her personally. Last
summer, Shirley had been more concerned with gardening
than soothsaying, and Miz Bonesteel was known to have the

greenest thumb in the community. People claimed she could grow roses in the middle of the interstate, if she had a mind to, and unlike her gift of the Sight, she was glad to talk about plants, and she was generous with cuttings and advice on how best to make your garden flourish. Shirley had Nora Bonesteel to thank for her newly planted flower beds, filled with only local plant species. But when the Havertys' Christmas tree was felled by that nonexistent gust of wind, Shirley had remembered her neighbor's other talent and decided to fight local ghosts with local magic, if that's what it was.

When Shirley dropped by to invite her neighbor to visit, she was careful not to mention anything about seeing ghosts or telling the future. She wished that there were gardening matters that they could discuss, but in bleak December there wasn't much you could grow except kale, which Shirley didn't care for. In the end she gave up on the idea of small talk. She just asked Miz Bonesteel to come over for a visit to see what they had done with the old Honeycutt place. She tried to sound offhand about the invitation, but since she had already told her neighbor about the fallen Christmas tree, surely she would understand that her visit was meant to be more than just a social call. At least Shirley hoped so, because she had no idea how to broach the subject of haunting in a casual conversation. She bought an angel food cake and some frozen strawberries from the grocery store in Hamelin, thinking that if she served refreshments it would make it seem less like a service call. Like a supernatural plumber, she told herself.

Shirley drove the short distance farther up the mountain along the winding one-lane road, edging past bushes of wild rhododendron and pines, still green even in the dead of winter. The sky, the color of wood smoke, seemed to be draped over the top of the mountain.

"We're here!" she said brightly, and Nora, who had been a frequent visitor at that house for more than half a century, nodded solemnly.

The Honeycutt place was a sprawling white clapboard house, encircled by a covered front porch, complete with a porch swing and hanging flower baskets, barren now and swaying slowly in the cold wind.

Nora was remembering the house in happier times. Always conjured up by the Christmas season was the year when she was still a little girl on the Bonesteel mountain farm, back when her beloved Grandma Flossie was still alive. The early 1930s, that would have been. In those days young Nora's dark hair was cut in a bob like Buster Brown's: bangs and straight edges all around. She wore homemade dresses made from the colorful cloth sacks that flour was sold in, and thick, black woolen stockings. She went barefoot in summer, and for most of the year, she wore shoes only to school and to church. Little Nora had to take care of those shoes and make them last, at least until she outgrew them, because she was given only one pair of shoes a year. That's what Christmas was for.

The Great Depression had come to the mountains but perhaps not as hard as it hit the city dwellers, those who lived in cement canyons and concrete hollers, without gardens or woods to hunt in, but the folks in the hills had food and firewood, whether the banks failed or not. Many of the men worked in the railroad yard in town—the Clinchfield Railroad, now long gone—and that generation's grandfathers had laid the track when they cut the railroad's path over the mountains. In the 1930s, the trailblazers' descendants saw the railroad jobs become scarce, and the extra money they had counted on to supplement their farming dried up when the layoffs began. They generally had enough to eat, even through the winter, thanks to the women canning vegetables from the garden and storing apples in the cellar. If your table held a roast turkey on Thanksgiving, it was a scrawny wild one, shot in the woods on the mountainside. The rest of the time, they made do with a chicken once a week or so from the flock in the hen run and salt pork from the autumn hog-killing. Many a meal in those days consisted of nothing but soup beans and corn bread, but nobody complained, and to Nora, who was too young to remember earlier, better times, those lean years just seemed normal.

Christmas was a simpler holiday back then, too. Traditionally the mountain people, like their forebears in Scotland, had observed Christmas only as a religious occasion, without the gifts, feasting, and ornate decorations that began to appear in the early twentieth century. Charles Dickens had invented the modern method of celebrating the holiday with the publication of *A Christmas Carol* in the 1860s; before that, it was a season of quiet dignity. Old Christmas also lasted twelve days, now mostly remembered because of the carol "The Twelve Days of Christmas." The last day of the ancient festival—January 6—marked the end of the yuletide, and in the mountains of a century ago, people celebrated that day with an age-old tradition called "Breakin' Up Christmas." That was when all the community—at least the young and the young at heart—gathered in somebody's cabin or parlor for an all-night party. The local musicians took out their mandolins and fiddles and played reels and old ballads brought from Britain and every other form of musical merriment they knew. The revels ended at sunrise on January 7, and when the people returned home to resume the tasks of their day-to-day existence, the holiday was over: Christmas had been broken up for another year.

The traditional time for wild and raucous winter celebrations had always been the secular holiday of New Year's, in Appalachia as it was in Scotland. New Year's Eve was the time when the young men whooped and shouted and fired their guns into the air, in lieu of the store-bought fireworks, which nobody had. Neighbors gathered together to drink hard cider and homemade whiskey (even that word had come from the Gaelic; it was originally *uisge beatha*: the water of life). People forgot the word's beginnings as the centuries rolled by, but they never forgot how to make it. Revelers danced and made a joyful noise—perhaps a giving of thanks for having made it through another year. They shared whatever they could spare in a buffet of food and wine or "shine," both homemade.

One Scottish New Year's custom, not yet forgotten in Celtic Britain, had not made the crossing to the New World: *first footing*. In olden times, people believed that your luck for the coming year would be determined by the first person to cross your threshold after midnight. The best sign of coming prosperity was to be first-footed by a tall, dark-haired man. A blonde woman entering your house was a bad omen. Sometimes a dark-haired man would set off just before midnight, going from house to house so that he could first foot his friends and neighbors, thus ensuring their good fortune.

But not here. Not in these mountains. The ballads, the quilt patterns, and some of the folktales had taken root in America's mountains, but not the custom of first footing, and not the quaint old words, like *fasht* and *doddle* and *ashet*. Some things had been lost in transition. On this side of the ocean, the tradition for conjuring up good luck for the coming year was to serve black-eyed peas for a New Year's meal. It was now more tradition than superstition, but those who remembered—or thought they did—claimed that during the year you would get a dollar for every black-eyed pea that you ate on New Year's Day.

Nora wondered if the Havertys knew of the old traditions or if they brought other customs with them when they moved up from Florida. She took a last look up at the house, remembering happier times. Then she opened the car door and followed Shirley up to the porch.

The patrol car had reached the edge of the farmhouse yard, and after letting the motor idle for a minute or two, and getting no response from the house, LeDonne cut the engine. Most of the time rural folks would be peeking out a window long before a stranger's car came within hailing distance. But not this time.

"Maybe he's not home," said Spencer, when another minute had passed. He sounded hopeful.

"On Christmas Eve?" LeDonne shook his head. "Where would they go?"

"Visiting relatives, maybe? Seeing the Christmas lights at the Bristol Speedway; last-minute shopping in Johnson City; out to dinner somewhere?" But he hauled himself out of the car, slammed the door, and began to walk slowly toward the porch. LeDonne followed at a carefully calculated distance, keeping his eyes on the house and his hand near his holster, watching for a curtain to move or a light to go on.

What little peeling paint was left here and there on the house indicated that it had once been white. It was a two-story structure built perhaps around 1900. It had never been anything except a simple, inexpensive dwelling for people who didn't have much money. The house had seen better days, though. It had once been chalk white and kept in good repair, surrounded by a well-tended yard bordered with flower beds. Once, long ago, the porch boards hadn't sagged; the tin roof wasn't rusty and patched with a different color of metal; the yard had not been overrun with tall, brown weeds. Spencer thought of a dead body—a form that still resembled a living person, but now lifeless and decaying, past redemption.

When Spencer was standing about ten feet from the steps of the porch, he cupped his hands on either side of his mouth to form a makeshift megaphone and called out, "Mr. Shull? Anybody home?" He performed this long-distance greeting automatically without a second thought, and he would have done it even if he had not been in law enforcement.

The custom of "helloing the house" was centuries old, harking all the way back to Scotland and Ireland, where most of these people's ancestors came from. Over the water, strangers approaching the house usually meant bad news: your cow was about to be taken; or you were going to be evicted from your land; or the enemy had come to burn and pillage, perhaps to kill your family. When you saw a stranger coming toward your house, you got ready to defend your family and your possessions. Things were more peaceful for the descendants of the Scots-Irish in the New World, but old habits to ensure survival die hard. The lesson of caution was repeated in these mountains during the War Between the States, which was a four-year reminder of the perils of marauding strangers. A century and a half had passed since those troubled times, and now the approaching strangers were just as likely to be door-to-door missionaries or lost hikers, but by then the wariness was second nature to those on the remote mountain farms. Perhaps without even remembering why, people still felt a chill of dread when someone they didn't know started heading for their front porch. Helloing the house was a courtesy and also a sign that the visitor was familiar with the local customs. It ensured the stranger a warmer welcome. Sometimes it determined whether they answered the door at all.

A stranger would call out to announce his presence at a safe distance in order to avoid sneaking up on the inhabitants of the house and to show that he meant no harm. That wasn't strictly true in this case, Spencer thought, because he had the arrest warrant in his pocket. But at least the gesture prevented them from having a shoot-out with an anxious resident who might feel guilty and therefore defensive about something that might have nothing to do with why they had come.

Spencer waited, still a few yards from the house, giving the inhabitants another few moments to respond. He didn't want to cause an incident if he could avoid it by showing patience and civility. If he had to do this at all, he intended to do it as gently as he could.

A few yards behind him, LeDonne waited with his hand on his weapon. You never knew.

After perhaps a minute, a window curtain twitched, and a few cold breaths later the front door opened slowly and an occupant of the house emerged, easing out so that he only had to open the door wide enough to get past it. LeDonne relaxed a little, rolling his eyes in exasperation, but he kept his hand close to the pistol grip.

Spencer took a long look at the man who appeared at the door. "Maybe it's his son we're after," he muttered.

The elderly man toddled out onto the front porch, staying close to the door, as he peered out at them, blinking uncertainly. His features bore the look of one of the old families, the ones who had settled here when the enemy was the Cherokee, not the Redcoats. The old fellow was short, lean, and wiry—a description that would probably fit most of the descendants of those original settlers. Scots-Irish genes produced Steve McQueen body types, not Arnold Schwarzeneggers. This fellow on the porch was no movie star, though. With his furrowed face and the halo of white hair that sprang up amidst the bald spots, he looked like he had reached seventy the hard way. His baggy gray work pants were much too big for him, giving him the look of a scarecrow in cast-off clothes. The ratty old green sweater that enveloped him was not quite as old as he was, but it was close, and the carpet slippers on his feet were an indication that the old man had no intention of doing farm work today. For a few more seconds, he studied the two officers standing in his front yard, and then he gave them a beaming smile and waved for them to come on up.

Spencer nodded his thanks, but he approached the front steps cautiously, in case someone else was lurking behind the door. It turned out that there was someone else there, but it was a frail elderly woman, who could only be the wife of the fellow on the porch. She managed a nod and a tremulous smile, but she stayed just inside the door, her eyes on her husband.

Spencer shook the man's outstretched hand. "Are you Mr. Shull? Mr. J. D. Shull?" Still smiling, the old man nodded. "That is, are you the *only* male Shull in residence here?"

"That's me, all right. I feel blessed to see you. Merry Christmas to you both. Are you playing Santa Claus this year? Because a big old turkey would be mighty welcome here." He craned his neck to look at the patrol car, perhaps hoping to see piles of food and presents in the backseat, but none were there.

By now, LeDonne had joined them on the porch, but he didn't offer to shake hands. LeDonne never liked anybody until they gave him a reason to, and winning his trust was past praying for. He waited in watchful silence.

"I wish I was delivering turkeys; that would be a fine errand for this holiday, but I'm Wake County's sheriff, and I'm afraid we're bringing you nothing but bad news tonight, Mr. Shull," Spencer was saying. "And, believe me, I hate to do this on Christmas Eve day, but I hope you understand that I didn't have any choice in the matter."

The old man's smile faded. "What's wrong, Sheriff? Did the cows get out into the road again?"

"No, sir, I'm afraid that's not it." Spencer reached into the pocket of his sheepskin coat. "I have a warrant for your arrest, Mr. Shull."

Shull stared at them open-mouthed. "A warrant? Arrest? Lordy, Sheriff, whatever for?"

"It's a traffic incident, sir."

The old man nodded. "I see. A traffic incident."

"Yes, sir. Our information is that last week on Kingston Pike in Knoxville, your vehicle collided with a black Mercedes belonging to the wife of Senator Robertson and that you did not stop at the scene. I'm sorry, but our orders are to bring you in today for that offense."

From behind the door, the old woman gasped in alarm. "Knoxville? But—"

Shull turned to the half-opened door and waved for his wife to be silent. "Now, Norma, you just let me handle this. These gentlemen are just doing their jobs, and they're being awful polite about it, so don't you jump in and confuse matters. You're letting all the heat out, standing with the door wide open. Why don't you make us all some coffee? They must be awful cold standing out here with that wind on the rise."

His wife gave him a stricken look, but he smiled at her and gestured for her to go back inside. "It will be all right, Norma. I don't reckon they intend on taking me all the way to Knoxville tonight. Do you, boys?"

LeDonne said, "Not tonight, sir, no." He didn't see any point in trying to explain the intricacies of legal jurisdiction to this old fellow—not when they were standing on a cold porch watching their breath make clouds in the air.

Norma Shull looked as if there was more she wanted to say, but her husband shook his head. After a moment's hesitation, with perhaps the silent communication of long-married couples passing between them, she nodded and closed the door.

When she had gone, there was an awkward silence, which Spencer filled with the first thing that came to his mind. "Would you like to read the warrant, Mr. Shull?"

The old man stretched out his hand. "Well, maybe just a squint at it."

Spencer handed him the paper and waited while he scanned it. Since the old man was holding the paper at arms' length, and not wearing glasses, Spencer wondered if he could make out the fine print, or even if he could understand what the warrant said at all, since it was written in impenetrable legalese. But before he could offer to read the document aloud, Mr. Shull looked up and smiled, apparently unfazed by his impending arrest. His cheery attitude did nothing to ease LeDonne's vigilance; as he was fond of saying, "Crocodiles smile."

Mr. Shull sighed. "I reckon you got me dead to rights, Sheriff. You'uns are a-fixing to take me back to town then— just not to Knoxville. Hamelin?"

"Yes, sir, I'm afraid so." Spencer shifted uneasily, as another gust of wind swept over the porch, making the dead leaves skitter across the brown grass. "I'll be honest with you, Mr. Shull: on top of everything else, I wish it wasn't Christmas Eve, because that makes things even more troublesome for you and complicated for us. Everything court-related comes to a standstill over the holidays. It might take a couple of days to get you into court for an arraignment, which has to happen before you can get a judge's ruling on bail. Judges are usually scarce around this time in December."

Shull's smile faded. "So you're telling me that, no matter what, I'll have to spend a few nights in jail, even though I've not been found guilty of anything yet?"

Spencer nodded, feeling embarrassed despite the fact that none of the circumstances were his doing. He was no more than the bearer of bad tidings, but sometimes "shoot the messenger" was more than just an old saying.

Norma Shull reappeared in the open doorway, holding a wooden tray with three coffee mugs on it. She must have heard the last bit of the conversation because she let out a cry of alarm, but a moment later she swallowed hard and subsided into a tense silence. Her husband didn't seem upset, though. He was still smiling as he motioned for his wife to bring out the coffee. "I understand, Sheriff. You have a job to do, no matter how you feel about it, personally."

"Yes, sir. That's it. I'm glad you understand. Not many people see it that way."

"I reckon the long wait isn't your fault either. It can't be helped. Judges have to have a little Christmas, too." He sighed, taking one of the mugs of coffee. Spencer took one so as not to hurt Mrs. Shull's feeling, but LeDonne made no move toward the tray. His frown deepened, as if he suspected these two elderly people of trying to poison them. *Crocodiles smile.*

Mr. Shull took a sip of his coffee, letting the steam from the cup warm his face. "Now don't you worry, Sheriff, I'll go right along with you peaceably. I don't say I wasn't a hot-tempered old devil in my younger days, but as you can see I'm well past it now. Got too old for trouble."

The sheriff smiled. "I'm headed that way myself, sir."

"Well, I won't be any trouble, Sheriff, I said I'd come along quietly, and I will. I do appreciate you bringing up that point about my having to stay locked up awhile on account of the holiday causing a delay for bail and all because that's the part of all this that raises a troublesome problem for me."

Spencer heaved a sigh of relief that an unpleasant confrontation had been avoided. "What problem is that, sir?"

Mr. Shull pointed toward the lowering gray sky. "Well now, since you asked: I make those out to be snow clouds up there, don't you?"

Spencer glanced up. Dark woolly clouds seemed to hover just above the mountains. "Yes, sir, I believe they are, but we don't want to get stranded on the road back any more than you do. I assure you that we plan to be safely back in Hamelin before the weather gets too bad. I understand your concern, but I'm used to driving in all kinds of weather, and if anything happens we have a police radio that we can use to call for help. We'll get you there safely."

Shull rubbed his chin as he considered the matter. "Well, Sheriff, you've done me a kindness by explaining the court situation and by trying to set my mind at rest about the drive. I'm sure I'd be safe in your hands." He sighed and shook his head. "But getting to town safely was not exactly what I was worrying about."

At the edge of the porch, LeDonne looked up, suddenly alert. His hand strayed to his holster, and he glared at the prisoner through narrowed eyes. *Here comes trouble,* he thought.

4

Nora Bonesteel took a last deep breath of the cold mountain air, before she went into the house, which would be overheated—but what would it look like? And would seeing it disturb her memories of the house from her youth? Shirley Haverty, who had already opened the front door, motioned for her to come in. Well, there was no help for it. She had promised, and she knew that she would have to see the house sometime, and now was as good a time as any.

Nora expected many changes and modernizations inside, and that was fine. The past was no place to live in. She just hoped that the Havertys were not like some of the new people, the ones she thought of as *displaced persons*: people who had moved to the mountains of east Tennessee but seemed to think they were in New Mexico.

These confused newcomers decorated their houses in desert hues: sand color, orange, and turquoise. Navajo flute music played on the stereo, and desert scene artwork hung on the walls. Little bitty potted cacti passed for houseplants. Nora didn't think that there was anything wrong with admiring New Mexico—for many people it might be a beautiful place, but if it was as flat and treeless as it looked in the pictures she had seen, she thought she might last a week there, at best, before the longing for green mountains began to feel like thirst. She did wonder why the folks who apparently loved the western desert country so much had tried to drag it all the way to Tennessee. Why didn't they just move *there*, instead of sitting on a forested mountain in east Tennessee, pretending that they were out West. Nora really wanted to know why they did this, but she doubted that she ever would, being too polite to bring up the matter with the displaced people she hardly knew. Still, she supposed that their décor was none of her business; after all, the houses were theirs, not hers. The eleventh commandment in the mountain South was: "Keep yourself to yourself." You didn't go meddling in other people's lives unless they flat-out asked you to, and sometimes not even then.

She paused for a moment in the hall. While she waited for her hostess to divest herself of scarf, gloves, and heavy coat, she studied the hall to see if it bore any resemblance to the room she had known as a girl.

There were differences, of course: tastes change over time; much of the original character remained, only the old feelings of warmth and harmony were gone. The old oak floor was still there and well cared for, not covered by wall-to-wall carpet. The dark, wooden hall stand just inside the front door was different from the old one, but its simple design matched the age of the house. On top of it, a wreath encircled a scented white candle, just where one had been in the old days. It made her sad, though, that this new store-bought table was some kind of veneer over pine or cardboard or whatever they used these days instead of the solid oak and chestnut furniture she remembered from years ago, which had been made by people you knew. She knew about wood. When her father was a young man, the timber boom had been big business in the mountains.

Before she was born, her father had worked in a logging camp, and because of it—or perhaps in spite of it—he had developed a love of all the different woods that grew in the mountains. He had never showed any skill as a woodcarver, but he did try his hand at making plain furniture from the beautiful mountain hardwoods: walnut, oak, maple, elm, and chestnut. Selling those pieces for a couple of dollars had brought in a little money for the family when times were hard, but some of her father's favorites the family had kept. The little cherrywood table that stood by the sofa in Nora's parlor had been made by him. Every time she polished the table with beeswax, she remembered her father making it. As a child, Nora had played in the tool-strewn room in the barn while her father worked. There the floor was covered in sawdust and wood shavings instead of straw, and instead of cow smells, there was a musky scent of lemon oil, beeswax, and newly planed wood.

While her father worked, he would talk to Nora about wood. Learning to tell one wood from another became a game for her. After a while she could tell them apart, both in their natural forms and again after the boards had been finished and polished to a mirror shine: the rich dark brown of walnut; the deep red of cherry; the white or pale yellow hues of maple—it was red, too, sometimes when it was finished, but easily distinguishable from cherrywood if you knew what to look for. The mellow golds of oak and chestnut were also similar in color but different in grain. *Chestnut* . . . the thought of it hurt like a sudden memory of a friend who had died young.

Well, time went on, and you couldn't wish it back. In Nora's youth, the great towering American chestnut trees were still a common sight; back then she had never thought to outlive them.

Hickory and ash and oak. A line from an old rhyme that her father sang sometimes when he worked. *Oak, ash, and thorn* . . . The lucky trees, he had called them, because by now everyone had forgotten that the phrase was a remnant of an even older adage, brought to the hills from Britain, naming the trees that long-ago people thought were magic. Folk said that if you planted a rowan tree—that is, a mountain ash—beside your front door, then evil could not cross your threshold. All these trees had flourished in the highland forests, and once upon a time, soaring above all of them was the king of the wood: the mighty chestnut.

By the early twentieth century, the timber barons who descended like locusts on the Southern mountains had cut down all the old-growth hardwoods that had stood for centuries, leaving the smaller ones to take their place, alongside the weed trees: locust, sumac, and that misnamed interloper, *the tree of heaven.*

You could still find some of the old solid wood furniture in antique shops or country auctions, if you knew what to look for, but you would pay a pretty penny for a side table that might have cost two dollars back when it was new. Nora doubted whether anyone would ever again have a new table built from the lumber of a living American chestnut, at least not within her lifetime. The trees were gone now. A plant disease called the chestnut blight, newly arrived in the wind from imported trees up north, had reached the mountains about the same time as the Great Depression. Forest by forest those soaring wooden giants began to sicken and die. The chestnuts went away, but the disease never did. Sometimes a new sapling would emerge from the forest soil near the remains of one of those long-dead trees. In ten years, the little tree might even reach broom height or higher, but by then it was already dying.

Always the blight swept in and enveloped it. Seeing a doomed and shriveled sapling made Nora think of the last verse of an old English ballad, *"And death put an end to his growing."*

The extermination of the great chestnut trees had been more of a loss to the mountain people than just losing some pretty trees. It was long-forgotten now, but place names like White Top and Yellow Knob took their names from the chestnut trees that once covered the mountains, flowering white in the spring and bearing golden leaves in the fall. There had been so many of these towering trees that whole mountainsides would shine in the chestnut's seasonal colors. Now the trees were a fading memory, but the old names remained.

In the eighteenth century, when John Sevier was governor and east Tennessee was *The West*, the settlers had relied on the chestnut trees for feed and shelter. Back then, the staple of the mountain farmer was not sheep or cattle, but hogs: cheaper to feed, hardier, and more self-sufficient than the stupid sheep or the delicate cattle. From frontier days until early in the twentieth century, the local farmers would turn their hogs loose in the woods to forage for themselves, feeding on the chestnuts that covered the forest floor. It had been an easy and economical way to raise livestock, and perhaps the settlers did not realize what a blessing it was until it was taken away.

From the earliest days of homesteading in these mountains, people had made cabins and barns, buckets and barrels out of the rot-resistant chestnut wood. That lumber had outlasted generations of frontiersmen and their descendants. Two hundred years later, chestnut boards were still as strong and sound as when they were first made, but no new ones had come along for nearly a century.

Nowadays American chestnut wood is so highly prized and so scarce that enterprising local craftsmen dismantle old barns and cabins, salvaging the wood for new creations: tables, cutting boards, and sometimes interior paneling—for those who could afford it or those from the old families who inherited it. Chestnut floors gleamed in Nora's house, lived in by generations of Bonesteels, all the way back to those who came down the Great Western Road to homestead in these hills, when it was still Cherokee country.

Nora felt Shirley Haverty touch her arm. "Are you all right, Miz Bonesteel?"

She nodded. "I was woolgathering. This time of year seems to bring it on."

"Come into the living room and meet Bill."

Nora had steeled herself to smile, no matter what they had done to the parlor, but when she crossed the threshold and looked around, her smile was genuine. Instead of the chrome and steel furniture she had been dreading, she saw flowered chintz sofas on either side of a blazing wood fire—not electric logs. The dark, wooden side tables gleamed and smelled of lemon polish, and between the small Oriental carpets the parlor's original oak floor—the one she had danced upon all those years ago—was refinished and polished to a golden shine. It wasn't the old days, but it honored their memory. She thought the judge's family and his long-dead neighbors could feel at home here.

Then she turned and saw the Christmas tree.

The wind smelled of snow. It shook the bare branches of the oaks and rattled the windows in the old farmhouse. On the sagging porch, Spencer's cheeks reddened in the cold, and LeDonne turned his back to the wind, but right now in terms of their concerns, the weather came in a distant second.

When Mr. Shull said that there was one thing about his arrest that he found troublesome, the sheriff willed himself not to groan. Just when you think you're going to have an easy time of an unpleasant job, some trivial matter always comes up, turning the simple task into a tangled mess. He hoped that Mr. Shull's problem, whatever it was, would turn out to be something he could solve—preferably in two minutes' time. The snow clouds seemed lower, and the three men were burning daylight, idling on the porch in the bone-chilling wind.

Spencer resolved to be patient with the old man. "What's troubling you, Mr. Shull? You won't be locked up in a cell with any other prisoners, so you needn't worry about your safety on that account. And before we leave here, we'll give you time to pack clothes and a toothbrush. You might take a book along to pass the time." Shull didn't look like a big reader, but Spencer had made the suggestion anyway, just in case. People could surprise you.

Shull glanced back at the half-open door. "Well, Sheriff, don't you worry about me. I'll be all right. I was in the war— Korea—not the big one; that was my daddy's war—but it was bad enough. I reckon I've been in worse places than a nice, clean Tennessee jail."

LeDonne, who had served in Vietnam, and brought some of it home with him, looked at the old man with more interest, but then he shrugged and went back to watching the half-open door.

"The plain truth of it is that what troubles me about all this is Norma," Shull was saying. "We live alone here on the farm, just the two of us, and we've been man and wife purt near fifty years by now. I keep things going about the place as best I can, but I'm not as spry as I used to be, and Norma has the arthritis awful bad. It's worse in the winter, when the cold just seems to settle in your bones." Tears welled in the old man's eyes, and he sighed.

"I'm truly sorry, sir," said Spencer, feeling more like Scrooge every minute. LeDonne remained impassive. "You know we can't take Mrs. Shull with you, don't you? You wouldn't want her to be in jail anyhow, and we sure wouldn't. But we don't want to risk her safety, either. Maybe someone can stay with her. Do you have any neighbors or kinfolk nearby that could take her in for a few days?"

Shull gave them a sad smile. "Bless you, no, Sheriff. I surely wish we did, but sad to say all our old friends have mostly passed, and what kinfolk we do have still living are the younger generations that we hardly know at all—haven't seen them in twenty years—and even they are long gone to places like Ohio and Dee-troit. California, one of 'em went to. Would you credit it?"

Spencer nodded thinking that if the relative out in California talked anything like Mr. Shull did, the entire state would need a translator in order to understand him. He was careful not to smile, though. His elderly Arrowood relatives, all dead now, had spoken much the same way. Their descendants, however, did not. He supposed it was the same for the relocated Shulls, just as it was at the Vietnamese restaurant that replaced the café in Johnson City. The elderly Asian-born owners still spoke their native language, along with some heavily accented English. Their twelve-year-old grandson, though, with his iPod and his Reeboks, understood only a few words of Vietnamese and spoke perfect English, give or take the east Tennessee accent. Old customs and speech patterns seldom survive for more than a generation in the homogenization of a big city.

Patiently, Spencer tried again. "Then how about one of your neighbors, Mr. Shull? Could they take her in?"

Mr. Shull's sorrowful expression suggested that he was personally responsible for his neighbors' inconvenient choices of where to spend Christmas. "Neighbors," he said with a weary sigh. "Oh, those farms that aren't for sale and vacant belong to the summer people, and you'll be lucky to see one of them back before Easter. We call those people snowbirds, 'cause they fly south for the winter. Now a mile or so past those places, you'll find the homes of people my age—places that have been in their families for generations. They'd help us if we asked them, but the fact is they're not here to ask. Come the holidays, they all head off to Cincinnati and points north and west of there, a-visiting with the children and the grandbabies. None of the young folks stay put anymore. Ever noticed that? Just like our kinfolk. Haven't seen hide nor hair of them for donkey's years. Kept thinking they'd come back one of these days, like their grandfathers did fifty years ago when they retired from the automobile factory, but these younger ones haven't come back even to visit."

Spencer glanced at LeDonne, hoping that the deputy could come up with another alternative, but LeDonne remained stone-faced and silent. Prisoners' troubles did not interest him, much less the woes of their wives and children. The family matters of arrestees were *their* problem, not his. If you asked him, he would say that felons ought to consider the welfare of their families before they break the law and get themselves locked up for it. Of course, criminals aren't known for forward thinking. Nobody ever thinks they'll get caught.

For one charitable but impulsive moment, Spencer thought of asking his mother if she could take old Mrs. Shull in for a few days. Widowed twenty years ago, Jane Arrowood now lived alone. That left plenty of room for guests in the trim white house on Elm Avenue, the home he'd grown up in. The sheriff dismissed that rash idea almost as soon it occurred to him, and fortunately, before he opened his mouth to suggest it. You don't go wishing strangers on your own relatives at Christmastime, especially if the people in need were related to prisoners that you didn't know, either. These days it wasn't safe. His mother was in good health, but she wasn't all that young herself anymore, and doing a good deed for Mrs. Shull might be completely safe, but it would also be an unwanted imposition on Jane Arrowood. You can't make people do good deeds for you—the one gesture canceled out the other.

Spencer was just wondering if he could persuade one of Hamelin's churches to come to the rescue when Shull spoke up again, still solemn and apologetic.

"I appreciate your concern, Sheriff. It does you credit, and it shows the true spirit of Christmas—well, not peace on earth, but goodwill towards men, anyhow. The thing is my Norma doesn't much like leaving home these days, especially not when the weather's bad. Her arthritis acts up something fierce when it's cold. Besides, if the fire went out in the house, the water pipes would freeze, for sure, and you know what that means. Busted pipes, and no water till you get 'em fixed . . ." He paused for breath and smiled again. "But don't you worry. I think Norma could manage here by herself for a couple of days, if the—" He broke off suddenly; his face went ashen, and the words seemed to curdle in his throat.

Oh, lord, not a heart attack, Spencer was thinking, but as soon as worries about cell-phone signals and images of the rescue squad flashed through his mind, he saw that the old man seemed to have recovered from whatever it was. He wasn't all right, though—he still had the sorrowful look of one whose troubles had just multiplied.

"I just remembered that darned wood pile." Shull pointed to a knee-high stack of cut-up logs piled up a little way from the house. "It's mighty small, ain't it, boys?"

Spencer nodded. At this time of year, most people had three or four times that much wood chopped, even if they had central heating. Although the town folks' fireplaces were mainly for decoration, it still took a truckload of wood to keep them burning through the coldest months. And surely out here, with elderly residents and no other source of heat . . .

"Where's the rest of your firewood, Mr. Shull?" He looked toward the ramshackle barn within sight of the house. Surely Shull would keep most of his wood supply in a dry place. You can't build a fire with wet logs. In winter—when you most needed ready fuel for your fire—the damp days usually outnumbered the dry ones. Any fool ought to know that.

"The rest of our firewood?" Shull was shaking his head. "Well, there's a sad tale to tell. You're right, Sheriff, this here is a pitiful small woodpile for keeping a woodstove going in the dark of December. You don't have to tell me that. I know it. And, boys, I hate to admit this, but that little pile over there is all the cut firewood we have."

"But that log pile is only good for a couple of days' worth of fuel," said LeDonne, startled out of his imperturbability. He knew that the court schedule—or lack of it—during the Christmas holiday might delay the old man's return home for most of a week, and that the harsh winter weather would hang around until mid-March. It usually didn't snow in the Tennessee mountains that close to spring, but it wasn't unheard of.

Shull nodded in agreement, still looking sorrowful. "It's a pitiful shame, idn't it? 'Course, I was meaning to lay in a store of firewood while it was still tolerably warm for working outside, but I was feeling poorly myself last month—got a cold that looked like it could turn into pneumonia. It wouldn't do my health any good to be traipsing outside in that condition, not at my age, so I thought I'd best wait. And then just when

I did get to feeling better and ready to go to woodcutting, the weather turned fierce for a spell. You remember that freezing rain we had afore Thanksgiving, don't you?"

"Yes, sir, I do." Spencer couldn't say so out loud, but he agreed with the old man that it had been unseasonably bad weather for November. Nevertheless, the old man had spent two-thirds of a century on that remote mountain farm, and he ought to have sense enough to know that you don't postpone outdoor work much past October; it was asking for trouble.

"So what with one thing and another, Sheriff, I just never got around to chopping that wood. I meant to. Back in September, I did manage to collect a couple of logs from trees that fell in last winter's ice storm—they're out there toward the barn—but every one of 'em is eight or ten feet long. Big as they are, even if you could move those thick old logs, they'd never fit in the woodstove, anyhow. And Norma here, you know she'd never be able to shift them, much less cut them up. You see, she can't chop wood, neither, not with her hands so stiff and sore these days. She's not getting any younger herself, though she does what she can. Always been a worker, that woman. I reckon I'd worry myself to death sitting in a nice warm jail, knowing that Norma was freezing out here. Why, she might not even survive it. And I reckon murder is more serious than a fender bender. You boys wouldn't want that on your conscience, would you? A poor, sweet lady like Norma who never did anybody any harm."

Spencer opened his mouth and closed it again. In desperation, he had been about to suggest taking Mrs. Shull to a hotel (how would they enter that in the department budget?), but that still wouldn't solve the problem of frozen pipes. Who knew how long these two old people might be without water, or if they could even afford to get the pipes fixed if they burst? Judging by the shabby condition of the house, money was tight around here.

He sighed. Things were getting more complicated by the minute. He wished he had either sent LeDonne out here by himself or left his conscience at home. In that case, they'd already be back in town. But he was the high sheriff, and he felt responsible for his constituents.

Spencer looked at LeDonne and shrugged. They had worked together for so long that sometimes the silent communication thing happened with them, too. In the awkward silence, LeDonne heard the sheriff's unspoken words loud and clear. He wasn't even surprised. After a weary sigh for all the do-gooders in the world, the deputy gave his boss a quick nod. It was no use arguing with a do-gooder; you might as well save your breath.

5

Nora shook hands with genial, silver-haired Bill Haverty and sat down next to Shirley on the flowered sofa, a cup of tea balanced on her lap. She smiled politely as the Havertys happily reminisced about past Christmases in Florida, when their children were little, so that Nora's silence went unnoticed.

"And do you have any family, Miz Bonesteel?" asked Bill.

Nora nodded. You always had family. Just because they were dead didn't mean that they had never been. Besides, it was best to say a simple yes to such questions, in order to foist off the inevitable holiday invitations from the well-meaning people who asked her. They intended to be kind, of course, but such offers were too close to charity, which she would never accept. Besides, Nora wanted to spend Christmas as she always had. She thought she would be more alone with the Havertys than she would be on her own in her house, set on what had been Bonesteel land since 1791.

She tried to focus her attention on the pleasantries of her hosts' idle conversation, but she couldn't seem to keep her mind anchored in the present. She waited for a moment, hoping they wouldn't think to ask for any particulars about her plans for the holiday, and they didn't. They went back to talking about themselves.

Nora's thoughts kept straying back to the old days, to the war. *And that was in another country . . .* It seemed to her that getting old was in itself another country. Sooner or later, cemeteries weren't full of strangers mostly older than you were; with every passing year they began filling up with your friends and kinfolk. The grave gathered in not only people you knew but people who knew *you*. People who remembered when you were a dark-haired laughing girl with a head full of notions and red ribbons in her dancing slippers. There were fewer of them every year. Now that she was older than almost everybody around, people saw her only as a solemn old woman, and they couldn't remember her being any other way. Over the years, she had taught Sunday school to fidgeting little boys who had now become the town's lawyers, businessmen, and civic leaders. Perhaps for old people that was the consolation for dying—that you could finally be back among the people who knew *you*—your real self—because now everyone on this side of the Great Divide was a stranger, and all your contemporaries were gone forever. With each passing year, or so it seemed to her, you became more and more of a stranger in the place where you'd lived all your life; each year you seemed to care a little less about what was happening now to the people you remembered as children. The world seemed farther away, somehow.

That was one thing about having the Sight, though, which made up for the fear it caused in other people and the awkwardness of seeing tragedy before it happened: you didn't always have to stay on this side of death if you didn't want to. She couldn't choose whom she would see or what knowledge might be revealed to her, but sometimes it was comforting to be able to set things right for those who needed it.

But she didn't go to cemeteries. Ever. And when her woodworking father had been building a coffin, little Nora never went near his workshop. Even now she didn't go looking for trouble, neither here nor there. Part of being a good neighbor was to keep out of other people's business, unless they needed your help more than they needed pride in their independence.

The Havertys' genial chatter was still going on. Nora remembered to smile, but she was thinking, *Now what has set me to thinking all those solemn thoughts in such a joyous season?* She supposed it was on account of being in the Honeycutt house again, sitting there in that old familiar parlor, picturing *then* as well as *now*. There had been a raft of happy memories stored within these old walls—but sad ones, too. Even at a remove of half a century, it hurt to remember those times. To remember the judge's passing, and a solemn-faced infant laid out in his white beribboned christening gown, dead of influenza. To remember Tom Honeycutt.

When was the last time she had seen Tom? If someone had asked her, she supposed that she would say it had been on his last leave—1942, that must have been—before he shipped out overseas. In a way that answer would be true, and it was the sort of reply that most people expected to hear. She had never told anybody about the real last time she had seen Tom—here in this room . . . when no one else could.

LeDonne stopped watching the swirling leaves in the wind-swept yard and went back to scowling up at the slate-colored clouds. The sheriff had given him that look as loud as a spoken word, so he knew what Spencer was about to offer, but he certainly didn't intend to encourage it. *Do-gooders.*

Sure enough, Spencer stood there, looking reluctant and yet relieved to have hit upon a solution to the problem of Norma Shull. He rubbed one gloved hand across his forehead. "Mr. Shull, I take your point about this being a hardship on your wife. Seeing as how it's Christmas and all, I reckon my deputy and I could chop enough of that wood to keep Mrs. Shull warm for a week or so, at least until you get back. It wouldn't take more than an hour or so, would it, Joe?"

LeDonne didn't even dignify that with an answer. He just shrugged and hoped that they could get it over with before the snow began to fall.

The old man was beaming. "Why, Sheriff, you are an angel unawares. I'd take you both in for coffee and some of the wife's brandied fruitcake, except that those clouds up there tell me you don't have that much time to spare. As quick as it gets dark this time of year, I reckon you boys had better get started right now, before the snow flies. Now I've only got the one maul for splitting those big logs, but maybe one of you could do the breaking up while the other one uses the chainsaw to cut the wood pieces into stove-size chunks."

LeDonne looked at Spencer and sighed. "I'll split the logs."

The sheriff nodded. "Then about halfway through, we'll swap over." They both knew that cutting wood with a gas-powered chainsaw took less time and effort than splitting the logs with the maul. City people would probably expect you to use an ax to split logs. They'd see the wedge and the blunt-ended, hammerlike maul as pounding tools rather than devices for cutting. The secret, though, was in the tool's weight and the force behind it. A few well-aimed blows from a maul would split a log before an ax-wielder could make much of a dent in it. LeDonne thought that using all his strength to pound logs with a big long-handled hammer would be a satisfying endeavor just then, better than slamming his fist into the side of the house, which he had also considered.

Shull beamed at them. "The maul and the chainsaw are in the barn, boys, in that little tool room on the right as you go inside. Ordinarily, I'd be right out there helping you, but I don't reckon I'd be much use to two fine strapping fellows like yourselves—not with my bad back playing up like it is." The two officers were already walking toward the barn. Shull called after them, "First door on the right!"

Spencer went into the storage room and came out with the maul in one hand and the chainsaw tucked under his arm. LeDonne reached for the maul, and the two of them headed back toward the log pile situated midway between the barn and the house.

Spencer set the chainsaw on a log and was reaching to start it when another thought struck him: "I hope he's got gas in this thing."

LeDonne's customary scowl deepened. "Well, if he hasn't,

I won't be the one siphoning some out of the patrol car's gas tank when you run out."

Spencer trotted back to the barn to check. A minute later he reappeared waving a square metal can. "It's okay," he yelled. He hauled the gas can back to the log pile and set it under the nearest tree. "Seems about half full. I think it might take two tanks of gas to get all that wood cut to size."

Before he pulled the starter string on the chainsaw, Spencer said, "It shouldn't take long to do this with the two of us working, Joe."

LeDonne nodded toward the darkening sky. "Good. 'Cause we don't have long." With perhaps more force than necessary, he brought the maul down on an oak log that had rolled a few feet away from the rest of the stack.

Spencer looked back at the dilapidated barn. It was open on both ends so that the wind sailed through it, seeming to focus the cold inside. Dirty, manure-studded straw covered the dirt floor. Although they had seen bales of hay stacked near the big wooden stall that would serve as a stock pen, the barn was empty. "I wonder where the livestock are?"

Without a backward glance, LeDonne said, "Maybe there

aren't any." He didn't even want to consider the alternate answer: *somewhere out there in the woods.*

Nora had always thought of Tom Honeycutt as one of the grown-ups, while she was just a neighborhood kid. She knew both the Honeycutt sons—*to speak to*, as people said—but Tom, the eldest, was at least seven years older than she was, at a point in life when such an age difference was an impassable gulf. Tom had been a tall, sandy-haired, rather serious young man, who wanted to follow his father into the practice of law. When they met, at church or some community social gathering, Tom was kind to her, as he was to all the neighbor youngsters, never teasing them or treating them like babies, but while she admired him for his accomplishments and liked him for his kindness, she certainly never harbored any romantic thoughts about him at all. In fact, when she thought back on it, she couldn't remember a single conversation they'd ever had with each other beyond hello and good-bye.

Along with the rest of the church's congregation, she had

prayed for him when the war came and he enlisted. He went from law school to officer training school, making a last stop in between, furloughed home at Thanksgiving to say good-bye to his folks. After services, there was a farewell reception in the church's meeting room so that the rest of the community could wish him well. The women baked cakes for the occasion, and the long wooden table was laden with pound cakes and angel food cakes and the one Nora's mother brought, her favorite: devil's food cake with pecans embedded in the chocolate frosting.

Nora thought Tom Honeycutt looked more grown-up than ever in his army dress uniform as he stood between fourteen-year-old Rob and their parents, smiling and trying to balance a cup of punch and shake the hands of well-wishers at the same time. As she went past, Nora smiled and nodded to the younger son, Rob, who was close to her own age, and he smiled back. Rob was a nice enough boy, but she didn't think he'd ever catch up to Tom in looks or brains; perhaps because he was the youngest, no one expected as much of him.

As she walked away, she heard Rob tell someone that just as soon as he was old enough, he planned to follow Tom into the army and go to officer candidate school himself. Nora couldn't imagine what either law school or army officer school could be like, but she knew they wouldn't be one bit like the one-room schoolhouse where she and Rob learnt their reading and ciphering. At the beginning of the reception, she had heard one of the older men saying that if you had to go into a war, being a commissioned officer was the way to go. Though none of them had actually been to war, Nora's father and his friends nodded in agreement.

Nora spent most of the reception in a corner, saying little and listening to the girls in her Sunday school class talk about dress patterns and how to fix their hair and which movie would be playing next at the theater in town. Everyone stopped talking, though, when Tom Honeycutt himself made a little speech thanking them all for the farewell party.

"Thank you all for postponing your Sunday dinners so you could come and see me," he said, and people nodded and smiled. "I've spent the past few months getting told what to do by a string of short-tempered officers, so you all are a sight for sore eyes. The only order I've been given today is, 'Eat some more cake, Tom.' "

That remark drew a sympathetic chuckle from the listeners, and when it died down, Tom's smile faded, and he addressed them now in a soft and somber tone. "It's fitting that I was allowed to come home over Thanksgiving, because I surely am thankful for the love and support of my family and for the kindness of all you good neighbors. No matter where they send me, I'll take with me these memories of home. I'm sorry I'll be having to miss Christmas here this year, but I hope to see you all again on the one after that."

Judge and Mrs. Honeycutt looked on with solemn pride while people applauded. The men who stood closest to Tom shook his hand or clapped him on the back. The women kissed his cheek and wished him well, but in the far corner of the room, Nora turned away so that no one could see her tears.

"It won't do any good to stack the wood this far from the house, Joe. Mrs. Shull could never get them into the house from here. I thought we could stack them on the porch."

LeDonne noted the "we." He rolled his eyes but said nothing.

Half an hour later, when LeDonne had finished splitting about half of the logs, Spencer swapped the chainsaw for the maul, so that each of them did only half of the really arduous work. Compared to hefting the heavy maul, it was no work at all to cut the logs down to size using the chainsaw. Around them on the frozen ground, chunks of split wood and sawdust covered the icy grass like a dusting of brown snowflakes.

Finally, a tired and impatient LeDonne kicked the last chunk of trimmed wood onto the ground toward the rest of the fragments of oak and sycamore logs. He rubbed the sweat off his forehead with his coat sleeve. "Doesn't feel as cold out here all of a sudden, does it?"

"I'm too sore to care, Joe." Spencer set down the maul, hunching his shoulders and stretching his arms while he tried unobtrusively to catch his breath. "We've been at this for over an hour now. Given the size of that house, we must have cut enough wood to heat it for most of a week. But we still have to get all of it up on the porch so that poor Mrs. Shull can manage to get them inside by herself. Did you notice a cart or something around here? Anything we can haul wood in."

LeDonne shook his head.

"Okay, let's have a look in the barn when we take the tools back. There's bound to be one around here somewhere."

There wasn't.

Nora knew that she should have anticipated the Havertys' Christmas tree. After all, when Shirley visited her to ask if the house was haunted, she had warned Nora about what to expect in the way of holiday decorations, even describing the tree and the outlandish ornaments the couple had collected to honor and reflect the character of Florida. Yes, she had been warned.

Somehow, though, she had not been prepared for a six-foot shiny aluminum Christmas tree that was so . . . so *pink*. Shrimp-colored, Shirley had called it. "That's what makes flamingos pink, Miz Bonesteel—all that shrimp they eat."

The metallic tree probably went well with the couple's

tropical ornaments, many now smashed by some intruder and thrown away. Nora was willing to believe that there were places in the world where such a tree would be the perfect decoration for the holiday celebration . . . but an old-fashioned clapboard farmhouse in the east Tennessee mountains was not one of those places. Nora made no comment about the tree. She would be the first to admit that the Havertys' seasonal choices were none of her business. She wondered who did think it was their business.

The feel of the house had not changed. When Shirley told her about the attack on their Christmas tree, Nora had wondered if someone or something consumed with anger had taken up residence in the old place, especially since it had been derelict and abandoned for so many years. But she didn't sense any such disturbance. The Honeycutt house had always felt serene and happy to her, and it still did. That didn't mean that the house hadn't seen its share of worry and sorrow; from time to time, it had, because there's always some tribulation in every family, no matter how happy they are in general. But here the troubles had always been brief exceptions to the normal mood of the inhabitants of the house. The Honeycutts had weathered the trials of life together, and they had remained happy with one another and at peace with the world. The presence of Bill and Shirley Haverty did not seem to have changed that. They, too, seemed contented and calm.

Nora's reverie was interrupted not by sound but by silence. She suddenly became aware that the Havertys had stopped talking, and both of them were looking at her expectantly. Apparently, they had run out of small talk and were ready to broach the subject of the damaged tree. Had they asked her a question? She had been miles away.

"I'm sorry," she said, "I don't always hear as well as I used to."

Bill nodded. "It happens to most of us sooner or later. I was saying I suppose you've heard about the recent incident with our Christmas tree."

"Yes," said Nora.

"It got knocked over twice. Ornaments broken. But no sign of a break-in."

"Yes."

Shirley chimed in, "And the CD player, Bill. Don't forget about that. It wasn't broken. It just wouldn't play."

"Oh, electronic devices," said her husband. "Nothing they do would ever surprise me. But this business with the tree—that's harder to explain away. It's certainly strange, but aside from those ornaments, of sentimental value only, nothing was harmed. I'm sure we needn't be frightened by it, although a rational explanation would set our minds at rest. I told Shirley that the tree must have been knocked over by a sudden gust of wind, but she worries—"

"It wasn't the wind," said Shirley. "Do you feel any kind of a draft in here, Miz Bonesteel? Because I don't."

"A sudden downdraft through the chimney, then."

Shirley's stony expression said what she thought of that theory.

Bill Haverty sighed, "Well, whatever it was, Shirley seems to think that you might be able to help us get to the bottom of it."

Nora considered it. "I might be able to make it stop, Mr. Haverty. I will help you if I can, but I don't promise that I'll give you any answers."

"You mean you won't know what made it happen?"

"I'll know." *But I won't tell you* hung in the air, unspoken.

Bill squirmed in his chair, ill at ease with all these hints about unseen forces. Women's foolishness, if you asked him. Always making something out of nothing. Out of a simple gust of wind. "Well, what exactly is it that you do, Miz Bonesteel? Do you lay out cards, or look into a crystal ball, or do you light candles and chant? I appreciate the fact that you've offered to help us, but just what do you do?"

"Nothing," said Nora.

Mr. Shull emerged from the house just as Joe LeDonne was setting down his last armload of split wood on top of the stack on the porch. He was holding a coffee mug in gloved hands, but although he wore a heavy coat and scarf, the picture of readiness was spoiled by the fact that he was still wearing bedroom slippers.

Spencer struggled up the porch steps with one final chunk of oak log. "All right, Mr. Shull," he said between gasps for breath, "There's your wood chopped. There's at least a week's worth there, so you don't have to worry about your wife now."

"Thank you, Sheriff. That was mighty kind of you to look after us like that."

"Let's go then," said LeDonne, nodding toward the patrol car. "We won't need the handcuffs, will we, sir?"

"Oh, no." Mr. Shull's solemn expression radiated fortitude and resignation. "No, I'm a man of my word. I'll go with you right along, now that I'm sure that Norma—" He broke off suddenly, hunching over and biting his knuckle. "Oh, lordy."

Spencer sighed. "Now, Mr. Shull, don't you give us any trouble. It's time to go."

"I know it is. I know it." Shull kept nodding and glancing back toward the door, "And I wish I could say I was ready, but the plain truth is I can't see my way clear to go with you'uns."

LeDonne's scowl deepened. He reached under his coat, "Handcuffs then, Sheriff?"

Spencer put up his hand palm out—the restraining gesture that meant *slow down*. Willing himself to be calm, he turned to the reluctant prisoner. "What is it now, Mr. Shull?"

Shull hung his head and mumbled, "I just remembered. And I'm ashamed to tell you."

"Force yourself," said Spencer between his teeth. Little clouds formed between them as their breath met the cold air.

"Well, there I was looking at that fine pile of firewood and giving silent thanks that Norma would be warm here at home, snow or no snow . . . and that's when I remembered about the window."

"What window?" sighed Spencer, ignoring LeDonne's exasperated groan.

"Well, it's just a little one, but it's in the bathroom. The windowpane broke a while back; I think maybe a bird flew into it. Well, I put a piece of cardboard in the empty frame with duct tape to stop the wind coming in, and I was meaning to fix it properly. I had the tools and the caulk around already. I even measured the window and went to town to get new glass for it." Seeing the sheriff's mutinous expression, Shull hastened to add, "And I got the replacement pane. I did. I bought the window glass, brought it home, and set it down on a towel under the sink so's I could replace it when I had the time. And wouldn't you know it? The very next day the weather turned mild again, and then it just slipped my mind, what with the usual chores to get done and my ailments last month and Norma's arthritis. I never gave it another thought. And now it's turned just bitterly cold, and—"

"You didn't replace the window," said Spencer. It wasn't even a question.

"But I meant to, Sheriff."

"And now you've noticed that the winter weather has set in, and you've decided you can't leave your ailing wife in a house with a broken window, right?"

Shull nodded happily. "It shouldn't take too awful long for me to fix it, though. It's an easy job—or it will be, once I find my reading glasses so's I can see to work close up. . . . Now I wonder where those glasses went to? I know I had them last week . . ."

LeDonne sighed, correctly interpreting his boss's expression of weary resignation. No use arguing with a do-gooder. "Well, at least it won't take as long as chopping up that infernal wood pile."

6

"Nothing?" Bill Haverty looked at Nora and then at his wife. "I thought you said she was going to help us get to the bottom of this tree business." Shirley made a little gesture that meant *hush*. She hoped Miz Bonesteel wouldn't notice or get offended by Bill's plain speaking and demand to be taken home. With an invisible something wrecking their Christmas decorations, she thought they couldn't afford to make any more enemies locally, especially not one with ties to the supernatural. Maybe Bill didn't believe in intangible things, but Shirley knew that nothing and nobody in these mountains took well to following rules. She was willing to believe that around here scientific logic might get outvoted.

Nora didn't seem to notice her hosts' surreptitious agitation. She sat as calmly as ever on the chintz sofa, hands folded in her lap, legs crossed at the ankles, and smiling the faraway smile of someone who is unfazed by silence.

Finally, Shirley spoke up. "Is there anything we can do for you, Miz Bonesteel? Would you like us to put on some Christmas music?"

Haven't you already? Nora was accustomed to examining her thoughts before she said them aloud, and this time she was glad of the habit. Just in time, she remembered what Shirley had said earlier: the Havertys' one recording of Christmas music was a selection of comic holiday songs, most of which she had never heard of. This being so, there was no need to ask if they also heard the music. They didn't.

Bing Crosby. "I'll Be Home for Christmas." It sounded as if the song were coming from a radio left on in the next room, but she knew it wasn't. Radio stations didn't play the same song over and over again without interruption. A conversation or a television would drown out the sound, but when everything was still and silent, the song played on so clear that you couldn't tell the imaginary music from the real thing.

Nora remembered the Havertys, whose presence had slipped her mind. They were still standing there, frowning with bewilderment at her, as if they thought she might be ill or perhaps had taken leave of her senses. She looked up at them with a faint smile. "If you don't mind, I'd just like to sit here for a while by myself."

"I swear this bathroom is colder than the outdoors was." Spencer Arrowood's patience was wearing thin because they had to fix the window and because he had to keep his coat on while the two of them tried to work in the close quarters of the Shulls' bathroom. Watching his breath make clouds in the air didn't help much, either. "How can they take a bath in this place? It's like a walk-in freezer!"

LeDonne grunted. "Don't think about that too much." In order to set the pane of glass, he had climbed into the tub with the tools and caulk for installing it, because there was no place to put them anywhere else in the tiny room. At least they wouldn't accidentally step on the new pane of glass. LeDonne had wrapped it in a bath towel and set it at the other end of the tub. Now he was leaning against the wall next to the window, waiting for further instructions.

"You might as well stay in there, Joe. Two of us won't fit out here between the sink and the tub. I guess this is a one-man job."

LeDonne scowled. "Yeah, and I know which man ought to be doing it."

"Well, if it weren't for those snow clouds, I'd let the old fellow do it himself, but I just know he'd take forever, after spending an hour looking for his reading glasses, and then he'd probably end up putting his foot through the replacement glass. We don't have time for his dithering. Just hand me the tools as I need them. We're better off without Mr. Shull in here trying to be helpful."

LeDonne couldn't argue with that. He shrugged and blew on his cupped hands in an effort to warm them up.

The Shulls' only bathroom was a narrow afterthought of a place, set in a pantry-sized space down the short hallway that led from the parlor to the kitchen. A white claw-footed bathtub stood against the left-hand wall separated from the sink and toilet by a space just wide enough for one person to walk through. The one small window was at the end of the room, about ten paces from the door. Apparently, Mr. Shull had removed the broken glass from the lower part of the window before he taped up the opening with cardboard. He hadn't done a proper job of it, though, because the cardboard had come unstuck and was flapping in the wind that coursed through the empty space. Shull had also left small jagged edges of window glass still sticking out of the wooden frame. In order to fit the replacement pane into the window, they would have to remove those shards.

Spencer grasped one of the longer slivers of glass with his fingers and tried to pull it out. "This is the tricky part, trying to pull out this broken glass. I'm afraid it will cut me to pieces, and my hands will be so numb from the cold that I won't even feel it."

"Can't you use a hammer?" asked LeDonne, wincing at the sight of the sheriff pulling at glass with his bare hands, expecting to see blood at any moment. He was thinking that having to administer first aid would be the last straw in a day that was dismal enough already.

Spencer looked up, still holding an inch-long sliver of glass. "A hammer? Nope. A hammer would just shatter those pieces that are stuck, and then we'd never get them out of the window frame."

"Well, you're right about one thing: if you try to get all the glass out the way you're going, you'll end up cutting your fingers to pieces."

"No, I'm done using my fingers. I got all the bigger pieces. Now I can use my pocketknife on the rest of them. At least that's one tool I'm sure we have, because I brought it with me. The shards I can't remove with my knife will come loose when I dig out the old caulking that held in the old glass." Another thought occurred to him. "Caulking. Uh-oh. Hey, Joe, look at that assortment of window-fixing materials we dumped in the bathtub, and please tell me that there's a tube of caulking material in there somewhere."

After rummaging around in Mr. Shull's assorted pile of household tools that they had transferred from the bathroom floor to the tub, LeDonne stood up, waving a large unopened tube of caulking. "Here it is. You're all set."

"Not unless there's a caulking gun in there to go with it. We couldn't be that lucky, could we?"

LeDonne knelt and extracted the metal caulking gun from the pile. "It's a Christmas miracle," he smirked.

"Great. I just wish I had saved that miracle on a wish to get us back to town before the snowstorm hits."

"It isn't snowing yet," said LeDonne. "But it's colder than a penguin's butt, so let's hurry up and fix this window before we freeze to death."

The Havertys had looked a little uncertain at first when Nora asked to be left alone in their own living room, but after an awkward silence, Shirley gently patted Nora's shoulder and announced that they would be in the kitchen having coffee whenever she felt like joining them. Nora nodded absently and went on staring at the fireplace as her hosts tiptoed away.

After a moment, Nora looked around her. The room was just as it had been when she came in: the Havertys' twenty-first-century parlor with its mix of estate sale wooden furniture and brand-new upholstered pieces. She didn't see anything out of the ordinary; the Havertys had left and no one appeared in their place. But she could still hear Bing Crosby singing, with the faraway sound of a radio playing in the next room. Anyone talking would drown it out, but if it were quiet, and you listened for it, you could hear every word. They still played that song on the radio at Christmastime, but she thought that most people had long forgotten the original meaning of it. In fact, now that more than seventy years had passed since Bing Crosby sang it, probably the majority of people nowadays had never known the song's significance in the first place. But Nora had been young then, and she remembered.

Now she listened again to the faint strains of the familiar tune. The preface to the song, seldom sung anymore, spoke of someone seeing green grass and palm trees and wishing he was somewhere else: back home, with snow on the ground, and presents under a brightly lit Christmas tree in the parlor. In the year the song was first recorded—1943—that sentiment perfectly expressed the longing of thousands of soldiers stationed overseas in strange new lands and homesick for familiar things, especially during the holidays. Nora could never hear it sung without picturing a man in uniform somewhere in the Pacific, battle-weary and dreaming of home.

Her next thought was always of Tom Honeycutt, solemn and handsome in his new dress uniform, standing there in the church parlor and telling the assembled friends and neighbors, "I'm sorry I'll be having to miss Christmas here this year, but I hope to see you all again on the one after that."

That hadn't happened.

From the moment she heard Tom utter those words, Nora had known that his wish would not come true, but she kept silent. She never felt called upon to tell people what she knew that they didn't—not anymore. Mostly they wouldn't believe that a schoolgirl from the back of beyond could see the future, and the ones who did believe never thanked her for it, because the news she gave folks was always bad. It made everyone in the community a little afraid of her, wondering what she might know about them but wouldn't say. They acted as if she could call down the misfortune herself, wishing it on anyone she pleased. Nora grew to hate the feeling of people watching her, looking for some sign of coming misfortune. These people tended to stay away from her, as if getting too close would bring on trouble. Even worse were the people who did believe and were fascinated by it. They treated her like a carnival fortune-teller, asking her if they would marry this boy or that one or if some ailing relative of theirs would die soon. Sometimes grown men even asked her financial questions about stocks and bonds and interest rates, none of which she understood at all.

Nora tried to tell the curious souls that the Sight was not like reading a newspaper all spread out before you in clear bold letters. "It's more like listening to a far-off radio station at night," she would tell them. "The sound fades in and out, so that you only catch a few words of conversation intermingled with the static, before it goes away." Almost always, what you hear is not enough to enable you to make sense of what the people on the radio program are talking about, and probably nothing particularly important would be said in the few seconds you were tuned in. The Sight was like that: just a few garbled glimpses of things to come, but maybe not the things you really wanted to know. Nora might foresee a neighbor's cow taken ill and dying, but she couldn't change the cow's fate any more than she could stop the Japanese planes from bombing Pearl Harbor. She wondered if she ought to tell people what she knew and share with them any visions that concerned them.

The only person Nora could talk to about this was her grandmother. The knowing of what was to come was a gift that ran in the family. Grandma Flossie came into it at age five, about the same age that Nora became aware of it. Her grandmother told Nora that their first ancestors to settle here had brought the Sight over from Scotland when they came to the New World. Sometimes it would skip a generation, but it always surfaced again somewhere down the line.

It took Nora a while to become accustomed to it, even at first to realize that not everyone knew what she knew. Her playmates had imaginary friends for pretend tea parties and make-believe companions to talk to. Nora, too, had an invisible friend, but she could see and hear hers, even if no one else could. She didn't have to make up a name for him, either, because he told her what it was. Nora never mentioned any of this to her playmates. She knew they wouldn't understand.

If they believed her, it might make them angry that she had something they did not.

Once, though, she had asked her grandmother if she ought to tell people what she knew about the troubles in store for them.

Grandma Flossie shook her head. "No. Nothing would be gained by that, for either one of you." It was late afternoon and she was in the family kitchen, preparing the vegetables for dinner. When Nora asked her question, the old woman set down the bowl of potatoes she was peeling, and patted a kitchen chair, motioning for her granddaughter to sit beside her.

Nora thought of the spindly blonde girl in her class who didn't have long to live and how much the girl wanted to know what would become of her. *Anything is better than not knowing*, she had said to Nora. "But suppose the person asked you outright about what was going to happen, and she really wanted to know."

"We are enjoined against it, Nora," Grandma Flossie said, picking up the heavy King James Bible from the table. Opening it to exactly the page she wanted in the New Testament, Grandma Flossie began to read, "This here's the Book of Matthew, chapter 6 verse 34: 'Take therefore no thought for the morrow: for the morrow shall take thought for the things of itself. *Sufficient* unto the day is the evil thereof.'"

Seeing Nora's blank look, she added, "What that means, child, is that people have enough to worry about every day, without having to go looking for the sorrow yet to come. If you cannot change what's to happen—and mostly you'll find that you can't—then it does no good for you to rob folks of their peace of mind, does it?"

"But maybe if they knew what was coming, they could avoid . . . prepare . . ."

"Or else their knowing would poison all their days to come, waiting for it to happen. Leave them be, Nora. I don't know why we're given to know these things when other people don't, but I am certain that the Lord did not intend for us to torment people with it."

She added, "Besides—remember this—knowing is one thing and changing is quite another. It's no use telling people their troubles if you can't help them avoid it."

Nora took this advice to heart. In time she came to see that her grandmother had been right: *knowing is one thing; changing is another*. At first it was hard to keep from trying to help people she was fond of, hoping to turn aside the trouble that was heading straight for them. But after one or two small attempts to save a friend from sorrow—warning about the pet dog that would be hit by a car; that the heirloom locket would be lost forever—Nora had learned to let the future alone. Even small troubles were too painful to impart to those who would suffer them. Often when the sorrowful thing had happened, those she had tried to warn would be angry with her, as if rather than foretelling it, she had caused it. They would ask her why she didn't stop it if she knew what was coming. When Nora was a schoolgirl, she had lost more than one friend by telling them about things to come. She learned to hold her peace.

That was why, when she saw Tom Honeycutt in his fine dress uniform telling the folks at the church reception that he hoped to be back on Ashe Mountain next Christmas, Nora had to turn away so that even her tearful expression would not give anyone an inkling of what was to come.

After that Sunday reception in church, Tom had traveled by train to Camp Davis over on the North Carolina coast, and from there he shipped out to Europe with the rest of the outfit. He wrote often to his parents, keeping his messages vague and cheerful and mentioning places with strange names that his mother had stopped even trying to pronounce. Then one day the letters stopped coming.

A few weeks after that, Nora happened to be visiting the Honeycutts when the two men in uniform came to the door.

Nora was often there that autumn because Miss Ida had taken a notion to start a quilt. She settled on a patchwork pattern with an embroidered object sewn into each square, each one representing some facet of the life of her eldest son. The quilt was to be a gift for him when he came back from the war. She planned to sew an army insignia, the emblem of the university he attended, a little image of the house, a football, and a scene of green mountains to represent home. That still left eight more squares to be decorated, and she had run out of ideas, but since she had all winter to decide what else to sew, she went ahead and started making it. She couldn't send the quilt off to Europe anyway, but perhaps she could enclose a photograph of it in one of her letters.

Miss Ida's immediate problem with the quilt was not so much a lack of ideas as it was a lack of vision. Her eyesight wasn't what it used to be, and her hands were no longer steady enough to thread a needle nor to make the tiny stitches required for fine sewing. Each year she seemed to need more light, even to read the newspaper at arm's length. The close work of embroidery was becoming increasingly difficult for her, but she would not give up. Old age might be overtaking her, but she refused to surrender to it.

One Sunday after church, Miss Ida had asked young Nora to come over two afternoons a week after school—with her parents' permission, of course. Nora, the quiet, well-mannered Bonesteel girl, was the perfect person to keep her company while she sewed. More importantly, she had young eyes so that she could thread needles for her and do the sewing on some of the tiniest embroidery stitches.

Nora agreed at once. She would have been happy to help Miss Ida with her sewing, even if she hadn't been promised a quarter for each time she came. She liked the Honeycutts and was happy to do any of them a good turn. She hoped that being helpful in any way she could would make up for the secret she knew and could not tell them. But Grandma Flossie had been right about that: nobody could change what happened on a far-off battlefield, and there was no use making the family start their grieving any sooner than they had to. Her silence was intended as a kindness. She came a few days a week, while the afternoons grew shorter and the wind covered the yard with dead leaves, and hour after hour she sewed on the patchwork quilt that Tom Honeycutt would never see.

The afternoon had faded into dusk, and Nora was getting ready to walk home when the two men in uniform knocked at the door. Miss Ida sprang up to answer it before Nora could stop her.

"Just a couple more minutes," said Spencer Arrowood. "I've got the old caulking out. Now hand me the pane of glass—and don't drop it."

"Don't *you* drop it," said LeDonne. "You're the one who keeps saying your fingers are numb. If it was up to me, we'd have been back in Hamelin three hours ago."

"I don't intend to drop it, Joe. I doubt if there's another new pane of glass within twenty miles of here."

"Even if there were, they wouldn't be open for business by now."

"Sensible of them. It'll be dark soon—always gets dark earlier on days with an overcast sky."

"I know, but we'll be headed back to town soon enough, and at least now I won't have that poor old lady on my conscience for the next few days. I know you don't feel sorry for them, Joe, but I do. If Shull had hit some ordinary citizen's car, we wouldn't have bothered to come and get him until next week, maybe after New Year's, even, if we were short-staffed. But, no, the senator wants his revenge right now. I hate it when people use their money or their prestige to bully folks, and I know you agree with me on that."

LeDonne scowled. "I'm here, aren't I?" He picked up the pane of glass and held it while Spencer carefully unwrapped the towel that protected it. "Got it? I'm going to let go now."

"Yep, I've got it. I'll just set it in place. Get ready to hand me the caulking stuff, and put the new tube in the caulking gun. I'm going to need it in about two minutes."

LeDonne held his breath while he watched the sheriff fit the pane of glass into the window frame. Only when he saw it slotted into place did he relax. "The way things are going today, I figured the glass would turn out to be the wrong size. And Lord knows what you would have done then. Called the rescue squad to bring out a new one?"

"No use thinking about it. It went in just fine." He stretched out one hand, keeping the other one on the pane of glass as an extra precaution. "I'm ready for the caulking gun."

LeDonne handed it over and watched while the sheriff outlined the windowpane with the caulk. "Looks like putting toothpaste on a brush."

Spencer nodded. "I always think of my mother using one of those squeeze tubes to put icing on a cake. Except I don't need that much precision." He stepped back and surveyed his handiwork. "Last step: smoothing it down before it dries."

LeDonne looked down at the assorted tools at his feet. "Do you need a putty knife?"

"I just use my fingers. I just have to make sure it's smooth and even. Makes a mess out of your fingers, but warm water and a sponge will fix that." He turned on the hot water tap in the sink.

"I would have bet good money that there'd be no water," LeDonne remarked.

"Water's okay. I just don't see a sponge or a washcloth any-where." He turned back to a smirking LeDonne. "Just hand me that old towel they wrapped the replacement glass in."

"I hope it warms up in here," said LeDonne.

"I expect it will, now that the window is fixed. And we are finished playing handyman. Just leave the tools in the tub, and let's go."

They made their way down the hall to the front room. Mr. Shull and his wife sat in armchairs on either side of the fireplace, a good-sized chunk of hickory log blazing. They recognized it as the wood they had chopped earlier that afternoon.

"Fire sure does make a joyful noise on a cold night, don't it, boys? And we have you to thank for it."

"Yeah, well, the window is done. It ought to hold if nothing else crashes into it. Time to go, Mr. Shull."

"Past time," muttered LeDonne, ostentatiously looking at his watch.

His wife watched as he stood up and pushed his chair back

133

from the fire, but she said nothing, and her expression did not change. Spencer expected to have to wait for a prolonged and tearful good-bye, but Mr. Shull took his leave with only a brief smile and a wave to his wife.

"Better get your coat, Mr. Shull. And a scarf and gloves, if you have them. The wind is fierce out there, but the car will be warm."

"I'm right behind you, Sheriff. Rarin' to go." He made it all the way to the bottom of the steps this time. "By the way, fellas, when you were out in the barn getting the wood-chopping tools, did you happen to notice whether there was enough feed for the cattle in there? Did they look all right?"

Spencer and LeDonne looked at each other. Finally, Spencer said, "We didn't see any cows in the barn, Mr. Shull."

The old man looked stricken. "Oh, lordy! Don't tell me they've got out again. Why, they'll every one freeze to death in this weather. There's four of them, and Petunia, she's pregnant. Just give me a little while to check the far field and the woods, and I'll be ready to go."

After a long pause full of silent shouting, Spencer said, "Go on back in the house, Mr. Shull, but, mind you, this is it. We'll round up your cows, but then you're coming with us. I don't care what else is wrong around here; once we get your livestock back in the barn, we are leaving—all three of us."

Shull hung his head. "I sure am sorry about this, Sheriff. It seems like I've had more than my share of misfortune today, but you've been mighty understanding about it."

Spencer shrugged off the apology. "Let's go, LeDonne. We'll check the back field first."

The deputy rolled his eyes. "Oh, they won't be there, Spencer. Those cows will all be in the woods. I'll bet you a partridge in a pear tree."

7

After a while, the two men in uniform left, but Nora did not go home. After her first distressed cry, Miss Ida sank down on the sofa. She sat silent now, but with tears rolling unheeded down her cheeks. Looking at her, Nora thought that Miss Ida had aged ten years in two minutes. Nora decided to stay with her until the judge came home. More than once she offered to make a pot of tea or something to eat, but Miss Ida just shook her head and went on staring into space while they waited. When Judge Honeycutt came in, it had been full dark for half an hour. Usually in that case, he would insist on driving Nora home. Although it wasn't far to the Bonesteel house, he said he wanted to make sure that she got home safely.

Tonight, though, when he saw the stricken look on his wife's face, he rushed toward her, all thoughts of Nora forgotten. He sat down beside her on the sofa and took her in his arms, and at last, she began to cry. Nora slipped away into the hall, put on her coat, left the house as quietly as she could, and hurried away into the darkness. There would be no more sewing on the quilt.

Nora returned to the house a few days later with the handful of people who had come back for a reception after the memorial service for Tom at the church. Some of their neighbors felt uneasy in the presence of such grief, and others did not think they were close enough to the family to attend a reception at their home, but some of the Honeycutt relatives from Knoxville came, as well as Miss Ida's two sisters and a couple of cousins from her side of the family. Nora went to deliver a plate of deviled eggs made by her grandmother. "This isn't because they need anything," Grandma Flossie had said. "I reckon the Honeycutts could buy and sell the whole mountain if they took a notion. We're sending this food to them to show that they have friends they can count on, and maybe to remind them that in spite of everything they have to go on living."

"Why don't you come with me?" Nora asked her grandmother. Her parents were among those who felt too shy to attend a reception in the home of a wealthy family.

Flossie Bonesteel shook her head. "I reckon I'd be too distracting for you, Nora. There may be people who will want to talk to you."

Nora wondered what her grandmother meant, but knowing she'd find out soon enough, she took the plate of eggs, covered with a clean dish towel, and walked up the road to the Honeycutts' place.

No one paid Nora any mind as she slipped through the unlocked door and into the front hall. Miss Ida's brave composure was finally broken by the finality of the memorial service, and the weeping of the other women present. Their combined lamentations made conversation difficult so that the men stood around awkwardly, looking as if they wished they were somewhere else.

"It's Nora, isn't it?" said a voice from behind her.

Nora kept her grip on the plate of deviled eggs for fear that she'd send it crashing to the floor. Slowly she nodded and turned around.

The other person in the hall was a solemn young man in army uniform. His strained smile was intended to put her at ease, but his eyes remained sad. Nora glanced into the parlor, where the weeping continued, and then back at the soldier in the hall.

"Hello, Tom," she said.

He nodded. "Yes, I thought you might be able to see me. You're one of the Bonesteels, aren't you? And you do recognize me. Well, thank you for not screaming and running away, little Nora. I was afraid you might."

"You were always kind to us kids, Tom," said Nora, trying to smile. "I don't see why I should be scared of you now, just because . . . because . . ."

"I'm dead. Yes, I'm afraid that puts me at a social disadvantage, so I'm glad you came." He spoke lightly, to put Nora at ease, but his eyes were still sad. "I wonder if you would please tell my mother that it's all right? I'm—" He paused, searching for words. "Well, I have no fear or pain anymore. Mostly I regret causing everyone such sorrow, especially Mama. Could you tell her that for me?"

Nora hesitated. "Couldn't you let her know yourself somehow?"

Tom Honeycutt shook his head. "I tried. But she's all closed in." He glanced toward the parlor doorway and winced. "Will you listen to them carrying on in there? They're so wrapped up in their mourning that you could drive a Sherman tank through that room and they wouldn't notice it. I suppose I should feel flattered, but somehow the gesture is lost on me. But you, little Nora, didn't know me well enough to be carrying on like that, so I hoped that I might be able to reach you."

"I'm still sorry you died, though," said Nora.

His smile was more genuine this time. "I appreciate that. But the fact that we barely knew each other is a gift. It is because you're not hobbled by grief that I can get through to you."

Nora hoped no one would notice her out in the hallway and come to lead her into the parlor. Setting the plate of eggs on the hall table, she took a few steps toward the stairs, out of the line of sight of those inside the room.

"She was making a quilt for you, Tom. I was helping her thread the needles and all. It's a beautiful quilt."

"Is it? It might have made a fine shroud." Seeing Nora's stricken look, he hastened to add, "Best not to think about any of that, eh, Nora? It's all over and done with, anyhow. No going back. I'd like to say good-bye though."

"What do you want me to tell Miss Ida? How you died?" She shuddered at the thought of it.

Tom Honeycutt shook his head. "Telling her that wouldn't be a kindness to either one of you, would it? No, wait a couple of days until she's had a chance to come to terms with things, and then—I don't know—tell her I wish I could have come home for Christmas."

"How would I explain knowing that?"

"Well, say that you had a dream, and in it I said I was all right."

"A dream? But she might think . . . she might think . . ."

"That you were trying to make yourself important by thinking up stories?"

141

Shamefaced, Nora nodded. She would hate for anyone to think such a thing of her, most of all Miss Ida, who was always kind.

"Yes, I see," said Tom. He thought for a moment. "Well, I'd better give you some proof then. Tell you something you wouldn't otherwise know. That ought to convince her."

"What about the judge?"

Tom sighed. "I think we'd better let my father alone. He has very clear ideas about how the world works, and I think any message from me would be more upsetting to him than reassuring. Dad will manage to cope with his grief on his own. It's my mother who needs comforting."

Nora blushed and looked down at her feet. "I wouldn't want to have to tell her anything embarrassing," she mumbled, "like where you have a birthmark that doesn't show when you have clothes on."

"Just as well, then, because I don't have any such thing." He smiled. "I'll try to think of something a little less graphic for you then." He seemed to be thinking again, and then he said, "I've got it. You said she was making a quilt for me—"

142

"She'll never finish it now," said Nora. "She hasn't sewn a stitch since she got the news."

"Tell her that I want her to finish the quilt, and tell her to put it on the Christmas shelf."

Nora repeated it slowly. "On the Christmas shelf?"

"Yes. She'll know what it means, Nora. Just tell her that."

"I will."

"Good. And Nora—thank you for not asking me what dying was like or what it's like where I am now."

Nora looked at him wide-eyed. "Why, it wouldn't be fittin' to do such a thing, Tom." Nora did not mean that religious scruples would keep her from questioning him; she meant that, according to their mountain code of ethics, prying into other people's business was a breach of good manners. *Never take charity. Never ask for anything*—not even answers.

"You owe me one partridge in a pear tree," said LeDonne, pointing to a steep wooded hillside where Mr. Shull's russet-and-white Herefords had taken shelter from the wind. "Told you they wouldn't be in the pasture."

"Well, you'll have to settle for a chicken sandwich, Joe, because Chick-fil-A doesn't do partridges." The sheriff stood still for a moment, watching the cows meander among the bare trees. "At least there are only four of them. Our best bet is to climb up there and get behind them; then we can drive them back to the barn."

"In this weather, they ought to beg us to take them there."

The wind and the bitter chill had more to do with it than their ability to herd livestock, but within half an hour, they had managed to chase the Hereford Four, as LeDonne called them, back down the slope and into the field of dry brown grass.

"There's usually one cow who's the boss," said Spencer. "If we can figure out which one she is, then all we have to do is get her to head for the barn, and the rest will follow."

The boss cow turned out to be a burly, wall-eyed old lady who balked at everything these shouting strangers tried to make her do; but, after standing immobile for a minute or two, just to show them who was in charge, she began to saunter off toward the barn, because, after all, that's where the food was. Without a moment's hesitation, the other three swayed and rolled in her wake, and five minutes later all four were in the barn, penned up and calmly munching hay, ignoring their herders completely.

Spencer checked the gate twice to make sure the cattle could not get out again, and then he followed LeDonne back to the house to pick up the prisoner.

Shull must have seen them coming, because before they reached the porch, he was outside wearing his coat and a battered old Stetson hat. He stood there serenely waving and smiling as the two lawmen trudged up into the yard, conspicuously *not* returning his greeting. His wife stood as expressionless as ever in the doorway, watching them come. The wind swirled more dead leaves around them, mixed with snowflakes.

"I hope you've said good-bye to your missus, Mr. Shull, because this time, we're taking you in. No more stalling."

Shull beamed at them. "I wouldn't dream of it, boys. Man of my word, that's me, but could you show me that arrest warrant again?"

"It's legal," said Spencer, pulling the form out of his coat pocket. "Want me to read it to you?"

Shull shook his head. "Just want to check something." He reached for the paper, and, turning his back to the wind, he held it at arm's length and read the first page.

A few moments later, Shull looked up at them and smiled. "If I'm reading this right, it says here that the fancy car in Knoxville was hit by a white Ford."

"Yes, sir," said Spencer. "That's how we found you. Somebody saw the county sticker and enough of the license plate for a vehicle records check."

"Uh-huh. Do you see a white Ford anywhere around here?"

Spencer's eyes widened as he turned to look around him. There was no vehicle at all in sight, not even a tractor. And, since they had been in the barn and the back fields, he knew there wasn't one there, either. But that proved nothing. Maybe the car was in the shop or lent to someone else. "All right, sir, where is it?"

Mr. Shull shook his head sadly. "No use me having a car at all, Sheriff. State of Tennessee took away my license two years back. My eyesight, you know. And Norma never did learn to drive. These days, neighbors take turns ferrying us to town for groceries."

LeDonne, who had been hovering beside him, expecting an escape attempt, leaned over and tapped the warrant. "It says right here: *J. D. Shull.* You're J. D. Shull, aren't you?"

"I sure am, son. But I'm not *the* J. D. Shull. I'm *a* J. D. Shull, if you catch my drift. There's a raft of us Shulls around Dark Hollow." Since the two lawmen were gaping at him, bereft of speech, he burbled happily on, "Now, what with the mention of that white Ford and all, I reckon that the J. D. you have come after is Jimmy Dean Shull. He lives another half mile along the road past here. 'Course, he and Crystal are in Ohio visiting the in-laws all this week. You might try back after New Year's. I'm Jeff Davis Shull, myself. Now, Jimmy and me, we're probably related, if we took the Shulls' *begats* back far enough, but I couldn't tell you how. It ain't close, though."

Spencer wasn't listening. "But, if you knew you didn't own a white Ford—"

From the doorway, Norma Shull finally spoke up. "I don't reckon we've been all the way to Knoxville since the World's Fair back in the 80s, have we, Jeff?"

"Not as I can remember, hon," said Shull, smiling back at her. "If I was a-wanting to go traveling around, I believe I'd head the other way. Bristol. For that NASCAR race at the speedway over there in August. With all the traffic they get there on race weekend, I'll bet that for those two days little old Bristol is an even bigger town than Knoxville. But, shoot, I ain't been there lately, either."

"Why didn't you just tell us that?" said LeDonne, who was mentally flipping through laws, trying to find one that Shull had broken by deceiving them, but having no luck. "You knew all along we weren't looking for you."

Shull sighed and stared out at the barren hillside. Finally, he mumbled, "Well, here's the thing, boys. I thought you were angels."

"What?"

Solemnly, Shull nodded. "I did. You see, Norma and me had been worried to death over what we were gonna do about the farm chores, with the neighbors all gone this week. Like I said, they take it in turns to help us. We've been praying for deliverance from the elements, so when you'uns showed up in the yard, I just figured you were an answer to prayer. After all, it is

Christmas Eve." He clapped the sheriff on the shoulder. "And you sure have acted like angels today, helping us like you did, making sure we'll be all right. We are thankful for it."

From the doorway, Mrs. Shull spoke up again, "I reckon you ought to be heading back to town now, though. It's starting to snow."

As the two lawmen trudged back to the patrol car, quarter-sized snowflakes swirling around them, J. D. Shull was still on the ramshackle porch, waving and calling out thanks.

When they were out of earshot, LeDonne said, "That old devil played us. Wasted our whole afternoon. Can we arrest him for anything?"

Spencer smiled and shook his head. "Nope. This is our fault, you know. We wouldn't have made that mistake if it hadn't been for the weather and the holiday and all. Normally, we would have confirmed his identity, asked to see his driver's license, and inspected the car. It would have taken all of two minutes. But we were in a hurry to get back to town."

LeDonne sneered. *"Angels!"*

"Yeah. Now *there's* a case of mistaken identity."

"You don't believe him, do you?"

The sheriff shrugged, but he was laughing. "Joe, I'm gonna take it as a cosmic Christmas present. We didn't have to arrest anybody on Christmas Eve, and for once, the people we were calling on were glad to see us. It's not a big miracle, but I'll take it."

The music had stopped. Nora Bonesteel, coming back from her reverie, looked around the room once more, but no one was there. She spent a few moments looking at the new furniture and at the Havertys' few scattered ornaments, now resting against the bottom of the built-in bookcase. She shook her head. "I wouldn't have thought you'd still come home for Christmas, Tom. Not after all this time." She waited, but there was only silence. "Everybody's long gone, you know. They don't spend Christmas here anymore, either." *But somebody does.* She didn't know why a pink metal tree and flamingo and alligator ornaments would annoy Tom Honeycutt after more than half a century had passed, but apparently they did. He didn't seem inclined to discuss it, either.

She had done as he asked all those years ago. A week or so after the memorial service, Nora had stopped by on her way home from school to pay her respects to Miss Ida. They sat at the big oak kitchen table, having tea and cookies, when she finally summoned the courage to tell Tom's mother about her "dream."

She delivered the message in a faltering voice, finishing with, "I don't mean to distress you, Miss Ida, but I think he'd want you to know."

Ida Honeycutt nodded. "Thank you, Nora. You're an honest girl, no question about that. And I've known your grandmother since we first came to live on this mountain. You were quite right to tell me this"—she paused, looking thoughtful—"you being one of the Bonesteels and all."

"Did it make sense then? The Christmas shelf? I'm sure that's what he said—in my dream," she finished lamely.

"Yes, Nora. It does indeed make sense. Now hurry up and finish your tea. We have a quilt to finish, don't we?"

The Christmas shelf.

Miss Ida had finished that quilt a few weeks before Christmas, and the finished piece was beautifully embroidered, rich in colors, and lovingly stitched, but Nora never saw it again. There was no Christmas party at the Honeycutts that year, nor any in the years to come. For a few years after the war, Miss Ida and the judge would go to visit their surviving son for the holidays, laden with presents for the grandchildren, but they never again held a celebration in the house on Ashe Mountain.

Nora looked again at the Havertys' few remaining ornaments, clustered like dry leaves against the bookcase beside the fireplace. From the look of the fancy carving on top of it, she thought that bookcase had been built by one of the Jessups while the house was still under construction. And knowing the Jessups, Nora thought there might be more to it than met the eye. The walnut shelves were still in good condition, smelling faintly of lemon polish and beeswax. Now it held only a few books, a teapot, and some local pottery that Shirley Haverty had picked up at one of the craft stores in town.

The Christmas shelf.

Nora thought about it for a few minutes more, hoping that she'd be given a sign of what to do next, but it was not forthcoming. Finally, she went into the kitchen, where Shirley and Bill were drinking coffee and trying to look as if everything was normal.

When Shirley caught sight of her in the doorway, she jumped up, rattling her coffee cup so that it nearly tipped over. "Miz Bonesteel! Did you find out anything?"

"I know how to make the disturbances stop, but you'll have to do as I ask without expecting to be told why."

Bill and Shirley glanced at each other. "All right," he said at last. "What do you advise?"

"In a little while, I want you to drive down the road to the Jessups' farm. Do you know where that is, Mr. Haverty?"

He nodded. "We get vegetables from them now and then. Nice folks."

"Yes. Well, you go over there and tell Darryl Jessup to cut you one of those white pine trees they've been growing for the Christmas trade. Tell him I sent you."

153

SHARYN MCCRUMB

"A Christmas tree, ma'am? But, you know, we have one."

"It has its place, I suppose, but it won't do for this house," said Nora. "Something has been trying to tell you that."

Shirley gasped. "So the house is haunted?"

"Only for a couple of days a year, I think. All he wants is Christmas the way he remembers. I guess that's what we all want."

Bill Haverty had taken an old coat from the hook by the kitchen door. He pulled out his gloves. "I'll go over there now."

"That's best," said Nora. "And when you come back with the tree, you bring Darryl's grandfather with you. His name is Wilson Jessup. Tell him you live in the Honeycutt house and that I asked for him to come."

Bill blinked. "Wilson Jessup. That's the old fellow there, isn't it? The one who takes care of their garden? What do you want him to come for?"

"If I'm right, I reckon you'll know." She sat down beside Shirley. "While we're waiting for you, Mrs. Haverty and I will pick up all those ornaments on the living room floor and put them back in the box." Her eyes twinkled. "Then we'll drink coffee, and she can tell me about Florida."

154

Wilson Jessup, who was a spry eighty-six and would tell any-body so, seemed not so much to be aging as fading. His skin was the color of parchment, and his hair was wisps of white as fine as thread. Frail as he was, though, he still got around tolerably well, and his memory was as sharp as ever.

He had insisted on helping Bill carry the white pine in from the car, and together they had set it up by the front window. It was a well-shaped little tree, about as tall as he was, but since it held no tinsel or decorations, it didn't put him in mind of the holidays. Now he stood next to the fireplace in the Havertys' living room, shifting from one foot to the other, for fear that he had not succeeded in getting all the mud off his boots when he came in.

"Thank you for coming, Wilson," said Nora, solemnly shaking his hand. "I wanted to ask you about something, and I reckon you're the only one left who would know." She gestured toward the walnut bookcase.

The old man's eyes widened. "I'll tell you one thing, Miss

Nora. I know who built that there open cabinet. That's my daddy's work, sure as I'm standing here."

"I thought so, too," said Nora. "He built it before your time, though, didn't he?"

"He did. But he built one or two others like that over the years. He made my mama one for our sitting room."

"Beautiful work," said Shirley, running her hand along one polished shelf. "Imagine building a thing like that from scratch."

"I reckon my daddy could build anything if you showed him a picture of it. I used to help him in the shop, but I never did learn to carve as well as he did. I know something about these old cabinets, though."

Nora nodded. "I thought you might, Wilson."

"There's a trick to it. He loved to do different things, and the judge asked him to make this one special." Wilson Jessup reached out and pulled on the middle shelf. It swung open like a door, and behind it was another set of shelves. "I reckon the Honeycutts wanted this secret place for hiding valuables. They had some beautiful things, remember?"

"Yes," said Nora. "All that went with them. But this didn't." She reached up to the shelf just above her head and pulled out what looked like a bundle of cloth. Bill Haverty helped her steady it, and together they laid the bundle on the rug, and unfolded it.

"Why, it's a quilt!" said Shirley. "Look at that embroidery. It must have taken ages."

"There's something else," said Bill, reaching for a carpetbag about the size of a purse. Carefully, he pulled it open, and slid the contents out onto the quilt.

A rocking horse, a star, a horn, an angel.

A dozen intricately carved images lay on the quilt, dulled by age but still as sturdy as when they were made.

Wilson Jessup spoke up. "My daddy made them, too. Cherrywood, they are. Made one for every Christmas, until—"

"Yes," said Nora softly, "until Tom died."

Shirley had picked up the wooden angel and held it up to the light. "Who do they belong to?"

"They're meant to go on a Christmas tree in this room," said Nora. "And then I reckon the owner of them can see them every year. When he comes home for Christmas."

Want to know more about Sharyn McCrumb
and check out other great fiction from Abingdon Press?

Check out www.abingdonpress.com
to read interviews with your favorite authors, find tips for
starting a reading group, and stay posted on
what new titles are on the horizon.

Be sure to visit Sharyn online!
www.sharynmccrumb.com